Something was wrong....

The odd sensation stayed with her as she plodded down the long, empty corridor to her bedroom. She dragged in lungfuls of air, but the vague odor only reminded her of Mrs. Hamadi's apartment.

When she switched on the light and turned to the bed, she froze. In the middle of the spread was a square envelope. Abby's heart leaped. Steve. It was from Steve. He'd come home, found her gone and left some vital information.

Flying across the room, she snatched up the envelope and quickly slit the flap. Out came a folded sheet of paper—and a picture of a baby lying on a striped blanket.

Shannon! It was not one of the pictures she'd taken. It was a new one. Had Steve found their child?

But ashen eyes scanned the first line of the note, the photograph fluttered silently to the carpet.

"Mrs. Claiborne, you must quickly contact your husband if you ever want to see your daughter alive again."

Dear Reader,

Remember Abby Franklin and Steve Claiborne from *Life Line?* Well, they're back in *Cradle and All* with a new adventure. This story is packed with so much tension and emotion that we tossed and turned all night worrying how we'd get Abby and Steve out of the trouble we landed them in. Hopefully you'll enjoy their new thriller as much as or more than you did their first.

Even though it's the middle of summer, we've been thinking of Christmas at 43 Light Street. In fact, we're writing a holiday mystery titled *What Child Is This?*, with Erin Morgan (Sabrina's former assistant) and baseball player Travis Stone. Erin lost her husband during Desert Storm and is reluctant to love again, while Trav has a secret too devastating to share, and a life-or-death quest he must pursue. Together they'll unlock the sins of the past and open up a Pandora's box of deadly trouble.

Have a great summer, and when the winter holiday season comes around, we hope you'll share it with the women of 43 Light Street in *What Child Is This?*

All our best chills and thrills,

Rebecca York
(a.k.a. Ruth Glick and Eileen Buckholtz)

Cradle and All

Rebecca York

TORONTO • NEW YORK • LONDON
AMSTERDAM • PARIS • SYDNEY • HAMBURG
STOCKHOLM • ATHENS • TOKYO • MILAN
MADRID • WARSAW • BUDAPEST • AUCKLAND

Harlequin Intrigue edition published July 1993

ISBN 0-373-22233-5

CRADLE AND ALL

Directory
4 3 L I G H T S T R E E T

	Room
ADVENTURES IN TRAVEL	204
BIRTH DATA, INC.	416
NOEL EMERY Paralegal Services	311
ABIGAIL FRANKLIN, Ph.D. Clinical Psychology	509
KATHRYN MARTIN, M.D.	509
O'MALLEY & O'MALLEY Detective Agency	518
LAURA ROSWELL, LL.B. Attorney at Law	311
SABRINA'S FANCY	Lobby
STRUCTURAL DESIGN GROUP	407
L. ROSSINI Superintendent	Lower Level

CAST OF CHARACTERS

Abby Franklin—She was living a mother's worst nightmare and fighting with all her might to save her child . . . and her husband.

Steve Claiborne—How could he tell his wife the kidnapping was all his fault?

Oliver Gibbs—Steve's shady ex-partner had dropped out of sight; now even the CIA was looking for him.

Amarjit Singh—His followers called him the Lion; the world knew him as a ruthless terrorist.

Mrs. Hamadi—Would Shannon become the child she could never have?

Jason Zacharias—If his new security service failed, his friends would die.

Tang Wu—He used his military connections to pull off his black-market deals.

Shannon Claiborne—She cried for mama.

Chapter One

You weren't supposed to go into labor eight weeks before the baby was due. So Dr. Abby Franklin ignored the worsening pain in her back while she sat through her 10:00 and 11:00 a.m. appointments.

Repressing a grimace, she ushered Mr. Pasternak into the waiting room and assured him his agoraphobia was very treatable. When he'd left, Abby stretched out an arm, steadying her rounded body against the door.

Thank goodness she didn't have another appointment until two. She had started back toward the inner office when a sudden gush of warm liquid between her legs changed her lethargic discomfort to heart-pounding panic.

God, no! It was much too soon for the baby. She hadn't even planned to go on leave from her private psychology practice for another month. On shaky legs, she wobbled to the phone, dropped into her chair, and called Dr. Goodman. When she reached him, she started babbling hoarsely about being in labor two months early.

"Are you having contractions?" he asked, his voice a mirror of the soothing tone she so often used with hysterical patients.

"No, but my water broke."

That got his attention. The bottom line was that he wanted her at Freeman Memorial Hospital as soon as she could get there. She'd managed to stay reasonably coherent through the conversation. The moment she hung up, she choked back a frightened sob.

Then the first real contraction hit her, and she forgot everything she'd learned in childbirth class about relaxation techniques. All she could do was sag in the chair and wait for the wave of pain to pass.

Perspiration plastered her dark hair to her forehead and the back of her neck. When she was able to breath normally again, she dialed her husband's number. If he drove fast, he could get here in twenty minutes from Baltimore-Washington International Airport, where his company, Claiborne Carriers, was located.

Jan Monroe, his secretary, caught the tension in Abby's voice. "Is something wrong?"

"Can I speak to Steve?"

"He isn't in right now, and there's a shipment he wanted to inspect before it went out." The young woman sounded both apologetic and perplexed.

"I'm in labor. And it's so early. Please, I—"

Jan sucked in a startled breath. "Gee, I'm sorry. He got a phone call this morning and just took off."

"When?"

"At eleven."

"Oh," was all Abby could manage.

"If he checks back, what should I tell him?"

What could she say? That she needed her husband. With her. Now. And if he couldn't be here with his arms around her, she craved the reassurance of his deep voice on the phone telling her everything was going to be all right.

"Abby?"

"I guess he can't drive me to the hospital."

"Abby, I'm so sorry."

"Tell Steve to meet me at Freeman Memorial. As soon as he can."

Abby dropped the phone back in the cradle as another contraction gripped her middle. Grabbing the arms of the chair, she clutched the leather-covered wood for dear life. Somehow, she was going to have to get through this by herself.

When she could speak again, she phoned downstairs to Laura Roswell's law office. Noel Zacharias, who was now working there part-time while she finished up her law degree, answered.

"Noel, I've got a problem."

"How can I help?"

"My water broke."

"But you're not due—" Noel stopped abruptly.

"I need a ride to the hospital."

"You've got it."

Two minutes later, Laura and Detective Jo O'Malley burst through her door. Both were part of the close-knit group of women who worked at 43 Light Street. Not only did they help each other professionally, they were all good friends.

"Noel's getting the car. We'll go downstairs with you," Jo said.

"Can you walk?" Laura asked.

Seeing the concern on her friends' faces, Abby dug down into her own inner strength. "I'm fine. Just let me lock up." She pulled her key ring out of her purse and led the group out into the hall. Then she stopped short. "Oh, no. I've got three patients this afternoon."

"Don't worry about that. I'll clear your calendar for the next..." Jo's voice trailed off.

"The next two months, at least." Abby fumbled in her purse and thrust her appointment book into Jo's hand. In the lobby, she looked anxiously out the window. What was taking so long?

Finally the car zipped around the corner, and she started for the door several paces ahead of her trailing friends. With a sigh of relief she sank into the car's seat and pulled the door closed.

"I'll take care of her and call you when it's over," Noel told Jo and Laura. She guided the car into the midday traffic. "We'll be there in a few minutes, Abby."

Abby reached up to touch her friend's arm. "Thanks."

Beside her, Noel began talking nervously. "Abby, you helped me out of a tight spot a few months ago. Now everything's going to be just fine for you, too."

Abby hung on to those words. Not so long ago Noel had been through a frightening ordeal that had begun when she'd witnessed a robbery and murder. But she'd also been reunited with the man she loved. If Noel could come up lucky, so could she.

Noel was still speaking. "Your being pregnant has made me think a lot about me and Jason. A baby has to make a change in your relationship."

Abby didn't answer. She couldn't tell her friend that impending parenthood had put her marriage under a lot of stress. Steve's parents had been pretty rough on their kids, and he had been afraid he'd do the same thing to a child of his own. As a result, they hadn't planned this pregnancy. For months Abby had been walking a fine line between feeling deliriously happy and guilty. She'd thought she had time to help Steve get ready. Now—

A giant fist gripped Abby's belly, and she tried to concentrate on the breathing techniques she'd barely practiced. But this time the pain was worse.

"Was it bad?" Noel asked.

"Stronger than I expected. And longer."

"Maybe you should time the pains. I mean, the contractions."

"Pains," Abby whispered, looking at her watch. Instead of the numbers and hands on the round disk, she saw her baby's face. She'd pictured her and Steve's child so many times over the past few months. When she hadn't known the gender, she'd seen a miniature copy of Steve—a little boy with blue eyes, sun-streaked hair and a strong chin. Although she'd never figured out how a baby could be born with sun-streaked locks. Then the ultrasonogram had told her it was a girl, and she'd switched the image to one with her own green eyes—and Steve's hair. She hadn't been willing to give up the hair.

"Oh, Shannon, honey," Abby murmured the name she'd picked out weeks ago, her hand flattening over her abdomen and unconsciously caressing the fabric of her dress. "You're going to be all right."

"What?" Noel asked.

Abby flushed. "Sorry. I was talking to myself."

Another contraction seized her, making it impossible to think. The pains were getting closer. Too close.

She swallowed around the lump blocking her windpipe. "Do you think you can go any faster?"

"YOU'RE WASTING MY TIME—and yours," Steve Claiborne ground out as he whirled from the window to face the two men who'd been questioning him about Oliver Gibbs for the past hour. They'd said his ex-partner was in trouble and needed his help, so he'd shown up at Room 152 in the Quality Inn Motel and found two "special investigators" waiting for him.

The one with the linebacker shoulders was McGuire. The one who looked like a Doberman who'd sat on a lighted match was Driscoll.

Their IDs had said they worked for the U.S. government. Now Steve was beginning to wonder. The longer they talked, the more convinced he was that they were about as interested in helping his ex-partner as the devil was in Sunday school. Neither one had answered any of his questions. Instead they'd just been pumping him for information.

"Now don't jump to conclusions," McGuire cautioned. "Your buddy's in hot water, and you'd be doing him a big favor to cooperate with us."

"What kind of hot water?"

"We're not at liberty to say."

Steve scowled. He hadn't heard from his friend in months—which was unusual, come to think of it. What had ol' Ollie gotten himself in to this time?

They'd been partners in a Far Eastern air cargo business for three years before he'd come home to marry Abby. And Steve still owned a small piece of the business, since Gibbs had never come up with the cash to buy him out. That had been a sore point between them, because being in debt had bruised Ollie's ego.

When he was drinking, Gibbs could be an irresponsible jerk. But when he was sober, Ollie was a damn good man to have in your corner and a top-notch pilot. However, his enthusiasm for making a quick deal had landed him in trouble more than once—like the time he'd signed on to deliver a shipment of rare Thai artwork to a private collector. He'd probably suspected it was too good to be anything but black market stuff. Unfortunately, he hadn't found out until he'd been arrested that the items were stolen from Thailand's national museum.

What was it this time? Did he have something the Feds wanted back? Steve kept the speculation to himself. Twice Ollie Gibbs had saved his life, and he owed it to his ex-partner to find out what was going on.

Steve's gaze bore into McGuire's. "Who are you really working for? The State Department? The CIA? The Mafia?"

"Oh, we're legit. But National Security's involved. Just tell us where Gibbs is and we'll leave you alone."

"National Security?" He laughed. "Can't you think of a more original line?"

"It's the truth."

"Yeah? Well, it doesn't matter who you are, I still don't have any information." He was skating along the edge of the truth. Although he didn't know for sure where to find Ollie, he could make a couple of good guesses. But he wasn't going to tell these jokers anything until he knew what game they were playing.

"Claiborne, you better not be lying to us."

Steve didn't like the unspoken threat. "Or what?"

Driscoll's Doberman face sharpened. "You've got a wife to think about now. And a baby on the way."

"You son of a bitch." Steve took several menacing steps toward the man, his fists clenched.

McGuire jumped up. "Now cool down. He just meant you wouldn't want to put anyone else in danger by not cooperating."

Steve stared from Driscoll to McGuire, but he stopped himself from belting anyone. McGuire was right. Abby didn't need any more problems—like a husband in jail for assaulting a federal agent.

THE CAR CAME to a bouncing halt in front of the emergency room entrance. Abby fumbled for her seat belt, but she was too sick and shaky to make her fingers work.

"Better get . . . wheelchair . . ." she barely managed.

Noel looked at her in panic. Then she ran toward the building.

Abby closed her eyes, whimpering now as she tried to deal with pain and fear. When the iron grip on her middle loosened, she started to sigh with relief. But almost at once, another contraction started and began building to an almost unendurable peak.

A wheelchair appeared beside the car. A nurse helped Abby into the seat and whisked her toward the building.

God, it wasn't supposed to be this way. None of the books had described this kind of labor. Not so early. Not so fast and hard.

"I think she's in transition," the nurse called out as they cleared the automatic doors. "Better hurry." She leaned down toward Abby. "When did your labor start, honey?"

Abby shook her head. She was trembling all over now, her teeth chattering as she sped along in the chair. Hoping against hope, she craned her head, looking for Steve. But he wasn't there.

"Call ahead to the delivery suite. I'm taking her right up," the woman shouted to the desk clerk before turning back to Abby. "Who's your O.B.?"

"Goodman." Moments later, Abby heard him being paged on the P.A. system.

They were in an elevator, then a dimly lit hall. And Dr. Goodman was striding toward her, his white coat billowing out behind him.

"Dr. . . ."

"Everything's going to be fine."

The nurse rushed her into one of the rooms off the corridor. Someone else helped her out of her clothes into a hospital gown, and onto a rolling cart.

Quick, urgent conversations swirled around her. "Precipitous labor." "Fetal monitor." "Thirty-two weeks." "Get Wilmer here, stat."

"Willman?"

"Wilmer. The neonatologist."

Abby's hands clenched the sides of the cart. *Please*, she prayed silently, *please let my baby be all right*.

She felt tears stinging the backs of her eyes.

"It'll stop hurting soon. You're almost ready to deliver."

The tears weren't for the pain. They were for her daughter. But she could barely talk—and why waste energy trying to explain?

The doors of the delivery room *whooshed* open, bathing her in antiseptic smell and bright lights. Someone adjusted the table. Another person draped her legs and then moved equipment into position.

"I ... have ... to ... push," Abby gasped.

"Not yet. Pant."

Abby did her best to fight the urge.

Dr. Goodman came in, his face covered by a green mask. Quickly he bent to examine her.

The need to push seized her again. "I—"

"Go for it!"

Firm hands propped up her shoulders. With a satisfied grunt, Abby bore down.

"That's good."

When the contraction was over, she flopped back, exhausted with the effort.

The pattern was repeated three or four times. Abby felt exhilarated. Moments ago she'd been helpless to control her body. Now she was working to birth the baby.

"Here comes another one. Take a deep breath."

Abby gave it her all, feeling a tingling, stretching sensation as she pushed. In the mirror above the delivery table, she saw the top of the baby's head.

"You're doing great," Dr. Goodman encouraged.

With the next contraction, she saw her baby's head emerge. The next push delivered her shoulders. Then Dr. Goodman was holding a red, wrinkled little body.

Abby held her breath. Why didn't the baby cry?

A weak, barely audible sound made her try to reach forward. The same hands that had helped her up pressed down on her shoulders.

"Please . . . I . . . is she all right?"

No one in the room responded to her frantic plea. Instead the medical team was focused on Shannon. One of the nurses rushed the baby to the side of the room. Then a green-clad figure was bending over the baby, doing things that brought a wave of terror crashing against Abby's chest.

Chapter Two

"What's wrong? What is he doing to her?" Abby choked out.

"It's all right. It's perfectly normal," the nurse soothed.

Abby paid no heed to the automatic, reassuring words. An eternity passed as she waited tensely for the real verdict. Then the man who had been working over Shannon was standing beside the delivery table.

"Dr. Franklin, I'm Dr. Wilmer."

"Please. What about my daughter?"

"Naturally, her birth weight's low—not quite three and a half pounds—which means she's going to have to stay in the hospital for a few weeks."

Abby watched his eyes. The eyes told you when a person was lying—or trying to soften a shocking verdict.

"But her APGAR score is good, and she's breathing normally, which is always our biggest worry with preemies. As of now, I don't see any other major problems."

The terrible tight feeling in Abby's soul eased up as tears of relief began to stream down her cheeks. "Can I hold her?"

"She's going directly to the neonatal unit. But as soon as you're up to moving about, you can go down there and visit."

Abby turned her head and stared at the tiny new life in the little cart. Her daughter and Steve's. She wanted so badly to cradle her infant in her arms.

But a moment later, a nurse wheeled the incubator cart away and Dr. Goodman was speaking to Abby, telling her he was going to stitch her up. He worked quickly, and soon she was moved from the table back onto a cart of her own. Abby's eyelids fluttered as she gave in to exhaustion. Then a loud scuffle on the other side of the double doors brought her back to alertness.

"I want to see my wife. *Now.*"

"You can't go in there," a woman protested.

"The hell I can't."

"Call security."

"Steve." Abby's voice was weak, but it got the nurse's attention.

"That's my husband. Let him in, please."

A minute later, a frantic-looking Steve, his clothes more or less covered by a hastily donned surgical gown, exploded through the door. Under his tan, his skin was gray. And his blue eyes had the bright, menacing look of an animal defending its mate.

His gaze zeroed in on Abby. For a moment suspended in time, he didn't move. She watched his whole expression change from stark fear to apology.

"I'm sorry." The words were barely above a whisper, but she heard.

She stretched her arm toward him. In two quick steps, he was beside her. "I'm sorry," he repeated. "I should have been here."

"You didn't know this was going to happen."

He nodded tightly. "Abby, sweetheart, are you okay?"

"Yes."

"Thank the Lord." He seized her hand, but his gaze swung frantically around the delivery room and then back to her. "The baby. Where's the baby?"

Abby's gaze was riveted to his face. All at once she knew what her panic a few minutes ago must have looked like to the hospital staff.

"They've taken her to the neonatal nursery. The doctor said she's breathing okay, and there aren't any major problems, just her low birth weight."

"Thank God," he repeated, the words sighing out from the depths of his soul.

She threaded her fingers through his, clinging with all the energy she still possessed to the warmth and reassurance of his flesh.

FINGERS WOVEN TIGHTLY with Abby's, Steve stayed at his wife's side as two nurses moved her to a private room.

Impatiently, he paced back and forth while they made sure she was doing all right. Finally, the two of them were alone and he could lean over her, touch her face, smooth back a lock of damp hair from her forehead. He wished he could say everything that was bottled up inside him, but words had never come easily to him. Especially not now.

"Oh, Steve," Abby murmured, lifting her arms toward him. Until that moment, he wasn't really sure how she felt.

Gratefully, he sank against her warmth, pulling her gently to him.

"Abby. Abby." Then his lips were on hers in a deep kiss that shook him to his soul.

I love you.
I'm sorry.
I was so scared.
Forgive me.

He put the silent entreaty into the kiss—and felt her give him back the same heartfelt emotions. He closed his eyes and clung to her, wishing he could lie down beside her on the bed and gather her close.

When he finally drew back, he wiped his hand across his eyes. "Tell me what happened."

"It was all so fast."

She told him some of it, about getting to the hospital and being rushed to the delivery room. He suspected she was withholding the worst. God, it must have been awful. Frightening. Painful. He knew she hadn't had any anesthetic, and she'd barely practiced the breathing techniques they'd started learning in class. They probably hadn't helped her.

"I called your office, but Jan said you were out at some meeting."

"Yeah, *some* meeting," he muttered under his breath.

Immediately he wished he'd kept the observation to himself, because he knew she'd caught the odd inflection in his voice. "What's wrong?"

"Nothing," he denied quickly. "It's not important." He smiled down at her reassuringly. "Tell me about the baby. Who does she look like?"

"It's hard to say. She's so small, and I only got to see her for a minute." Her eyes grew misty as she tried to fill in the details he'd missed out on.

"I guess if we're going to talk about her we ought to give her a name. We should have discussed some."

"I—I know. But I've been thinking about it," Abby told him hesitantly.

"You don't want to name her after your Great-Aunt Hepsabah, do you?" he teased.

She dredged up a little grin, but in the next moment her expression became watchful. "No. I was thinking about Shannon. For your sister, Sharon."

He went very still, conscious of Abby's anxious eyes on his face. It had been more than three years since Sharon's murder; he still mourned the loss.

Experimentally, he tried out the name. "Shannon Claiborne."

"Would you...mind? Would it make you feel sad?"

"No. Shannon Claiborne has a nice ring. And I know Sharon would have liked it, too."

They were both quiet for a moment. Then, without warning, he saw something on her face that made his heart stop and start up again double-time.

"Sweetheart. What? What's wrong? Are you in pain? Should I get the doctor?"

Struggling to a sitting position, she gripped his arm. "I've got to see her! I've got to make sure she's really all right."

"Abby, you've just given birth. You—"

"You can make them let me go to her," she interrupted. "I saw how you battled your way into the delivery room. Not even that Amazon nurse could stop you. They won't stop you from getting me a wheelchair."

He stared at her helplessly. "You shouldn't be out of bed."

"Maybe. But I'm going to the neonatal nursery to see Shannon. You can either find me a wheelchair, or I'm going to walk."

Determination had stiffened every muscle in her face. She meant what she said.

"All right."

Steve turned toward the door so she couldn't read his expression. He hadn't been there to drive her to the hospital. He hadn't been with her when Shannon was born. Now she was asking something from him—and he was going to make sure she got what she wanted. Unless the medical staff said she was taking too much of a risk getting up so soon. Then he'd help them tie her to the bed if that was the only way to make her take care of herself.

He started down the hall, his hands clenched at his sides. It was easier to focus on Abby's request than on the reason why he hadn't been here an hour ago. Yet he had to think about that, too. He'd missed the birth of his daughter because he'd been in a motel room lying his head off to two government agents. If that's what they really were.

He shuddered. Those two goons had threatened his wife and child. And he was damn well going to make sure they were protected.

HE WAS NEVER GOING to get used to the tubes and the wires and the monitoring machines, Steve thought as Abby palmed the latch on the neonatology nursery door. Which was why Abby had been down here ten times to his every one.

Shannon was two weeks old. Neither of them had even picked her up. Abby could hardly stand it. She wanted to hold her daughter in her arms and nurse her, not just bring bottles of her milk to the hospital.

He was secretly relieved by the restrictions. If he lifted his daughter's tiny body in his clumsy hands, he'd probably break her.

He'd tried to act as if he was taking Abby's pregnancy in stride, but he knew he hadn't fooled her. And his fear of failure as a parent had grown worse as her body had filled out.

But until Shannon was born, the scenes he'd pictured between himself and his offspring had been based on memories of himself as a hard-as-nails seven-year-old. A little boy trying to pretend it didn't matter that he could never do anything right as far as his old man was concerned. Or of a twelve-year-old getting his hide tanned for running away. Or a fifteen-year-old who'd taken his father's Caddy and crashed it into a stone wall along Green Spring Valley Road.

Mostly, he'd pictured a large, angry man standing over a defenseless kid, demanding perfection.

He hadn't really thought about little babies. Or the responsibility of caring for a tiny human life so fragile that she needed to be protected in a little plastic crib, walled off from danger. Walled off from him.

Abby leaned over the isolette where Shannon lay and reached through the slot in the side, her hand cupping around the tiny head of hair. Dark. Like Abby's. Would it stay that way?

Abby stroked her daughter's soft cheek and checked the diaper under her. They didn't try to pin them on to a kid that small. "She doesn't need changing."

"Yeah."

Abby began to talk to Shannon in that soft, motherly way she had, and Steve glanced at the monitor, watching in renewed wonder as the baby's heart rate slowed. Shannon liked the sound of her mother's voice. Or at least that was what the nurse had said.

He came up behind Abby and awkwardly grasped her shoulder.

"She gained another ounce yesterday," she murmured.

"Yeah."

"We can bring her home when she weighs five pounds."

"Mm-hmm."

Shannon was staring at him with those navy blue eyes of hers. As if she knew all this was his fault.

He clenched his teeth and then glanced quickly at Abby, glad that her back was to him. He'd gone home from the hospital that first night and pawed through Abby's pregnancy books to find out what could make a woman go into labor. One of the reasons was making love.

She'd been tired the night before Shannon was born, but he hadn't had all that much trouble getting her in the mood. Even seven months pregnant, she'd been so responsive to him. Now he had reason to regret his selfishness. Good reason.

A silent curse knifed through his mind.

"What?" Abby murmured.

"Nothing. I was just clearing my throat."

He must have made some noise. Or had Abby heard his thoughts? Usually when he was troubled by something, Abby knew it and tried to get him to open up. He'd hated that at first. Funny how he'd gotten used to letting her persuade him to share the bad stuff as well as the good. But she hadn't tried to this time. This time she was too worried about Shannon. And he wasn't going to force any more burdens on her.

It wasn't just Shannon's premature birth that ate at him day and night. He needed to talk about the CIA and Oliver, to explain to Abby how he was caught between a rock and a hard place. He owed Oliver Gibbs his life. He didn't want to turn him in to the U.S. government. But maybe he was going to have to do it.

He couldn't lay that on Abby, either, not while he felt so damn guilty. Not while she was so worried. So he'd kept his mouth shut. And done his damnedest to make sure everything turned out all right.

ABBY EASED BACK into the rocker, wishing her hands weren't trembling. For three endless weeks she'd longed to hold her tiny, precious daughter. Now the moment had arrived, and she was terrified.

The nurse had probably been through this a zillion times. "There's nothing to worry about," she murmured as she placed the small, blanket-wrapped bundle in Abby's arms, deftly adjusting the tubes and wires that still attached Shannon to a bank of monitors and other machines.

"She's—she feels so fragile." In the next moment Abby gave a startled cry as a tiny fist flailed out of the receiving blanket and socked her in the chest.

The nurse laughed. "She been a fighter right from the first. And she's over four pounds now. In a few weeks, you'll be taking her home."

"Yes," Abby whispered, looking down into the alert little face that was still red and wrinkled. Shannon gazed back, regarding her quizzically with eyes that did indeed remind her of Steve's, although they were still the dark, almost navy blue of the newborn. The baby's straight, silky hair was also dark.

Abby touched a gentle finger to her daughter's petal-soft cheek, and the small head turned. Opening her mouth, Shannon began to work her lips against the finger. Then she started to whimper, the sound escalating to fill the small private room off the main nursery for premature infants.

"She's crying."

"She's hungry. Why don't you go ahead and nurse her."

"Oh, right," Abby managed, aware that her speech seemed to have shrunk to awed monosyllables. Awkwardly, she began to pull up the cotton T-shirt she'd worn for the occasion. Until now, she'd been bringing in bottles of her milk for Shannon. This was the first time they were going to do it the natural way.

"Hold her up a little higher. That's right."

Abby winced at the sudden, unexpected pain that flashed through her nipple as the baby began to suck. The discomfort lasted only a second. Then she looked down in wonder at the tiny mouth pulling on her breast.

"She's got to work harder to draw the milk from you than she does from the bottle, so she may not get as much at first," the nurse advised.

Abby already knew that. She knew everything there was to know about premature infants—or rather, everything that you could learn from a book. While Shannon still seemed tiny, she'd been big by premature standards. Three and a half pounds at birth, although she'd lost some weight in the first few days. But medical science could save babies as small as a pound.

Out in the nursery another tiny resident began to cry.

"I'll leave you alone for a while."

"Is that okay?"

"I won't be far. Just sing out if you need anything."

Abby tried to unstiffen her body. Her eyes went from her child to the other chair positioned across from hers. Was that for the father? So he could be part of the experience?

She'd told Steve she was probably going to hold Shannon for the first time today—and probably nurse her, too. Her husband had said he'd try to get here by five-thirty. But after waiting half an hour in the nursery, Abby had decided to go ahead.

She closed her eyes, playing a ridiculous little game with herself. When she opened them, Steve would be here to share this important moment.

It didn't happen. She'd been at the hospital visiting her daughter for hours every day since she'd been discharged. Steve had come with her some of the time, but it was clear he didn't feel comfortable in the neonatology ward. And it was also clear something was troubling him.

She knew he was worried because Shannon looked so fragile. He'd owned up to that.

Was that why he'd barely touched his child? Or was there more to it? Did he resent all the time his wife had been spending with the baby?

Abby grimaced. Usually she could get him to communicate with her. Over the past few weeks she'd tried once or twice, but she'd been too drained of emotional or physical energy to keep at it when he'd changed the subject.

No. That wasn't all of it, she silently admitted. Maybe she should have scheduled a few sessions with one of her colleagues. She'd worked with patients who'd been depressed after childbirth. She hadn't ever thought it would happen to her. But, then, she hadn't dreamed of all these added problems, either.

Well, in another week or two, she and Steve would be bringing Shannon home. Then they could get back to normal. But right now Shannon had to be her primary concern.

"See, you're doing fine."

Abby had been so wound up with her thoughts that she hadn't even heard the nurse come back. "Yes."

"Your husband's going to be sorry he missed this."

"Mmm-hmm."

"You probably want to switch to the other breast."

"Yes."

"Let me help you with the wiring."

"Thanks." Abby detached Shannon the way the books advised. Then the nurse adjusted the external equipment so Abby could burp the baby.

A few minutes later she relaxed back into the rocker, watching her daughter enthusiastically tackle the renewed milk supply.

When the door opened again, she looked up—hoping that Steve had finally made it. This time, instead of her husband, she saw Mrs. Hamadi, one of the volunteers. The East Indian woman had told Abby she'd immigrated to Baltimore several years ago.

"You're here early." Usually Abby encountered Mrs. Hamadi only when she made one of her nighttime visits to the nursery.

The newcomer stood in the doorway. Her face was unusual—long and thin, with heavy, unplucked brows. A red jewel decorated one side of her nose. At the moment her eyes drilled into the center of Abby's chest and the child she cradled in her arms.

"So you're finally nursing her." She spoke in a lilting singsong that Abby had found a bit difficult to understand at first.

Abby nodded. Feeling unaccountably exposed, she stifled the impulse to pull the blanket up around her breast. She raised her eyes to the woman's face, and for an unguarded moment, she caught a look of longing that made her heart melt.

Mrs. Hamadi fiddled with the ties of the kerchief that confined her dark hair. "Shannon is getting bigger. She'll be ready to leave the hospital soon."

"I've got my fingers crossed. But the doctor said she has to gain another pound first."

"And when do you think that will be?"

"A couple of weeks—I hope."

"That's good. Very good."

"You've taken such an interest in her."

"She's—how do you say?—special."

"Yes," Abby murmured, her fingers stroking her daughter's silk hair.

"Perhaps I will see you another time." Without waiting for an answer, Mrs. Hamadi turned away. Abby watched through the glass panel in the door as she strode from the nursery, her long, baggy culottes swishing around her legs. Odd that she'd just shown up like this and then rushed away. But then, she wasn't the run-of-the-mill volunteer. In the dark hours of the night, when Abby had come to the hospital to watch her daughter sleep in her isolette, the two of them had traded confidences.

Several years ago, Mrs. Hamadi had borne three premature babies of her own. None of them had been strong enough to live, and the grief over each death had been compounded by her husband's masculine pride. He'd been vocal about his wife's inability to give him a son, and he'd left her when the doctors had said she couldn't have any more children of her own. For a long time, she hadn't known how to put her life back together. Then, gradually, she'd learned how to cope. Now she worked in a cosmetics factory, ironically, since she never wore any makeup. In addition, she'd volunteered to give her time caring for other women's infants.

Abby wondered if Mrs. Hamadi had regretted revealing so much about her own life. After the whispered confidences, she hadn't spoken so intimately again. In fact, she'd acted quite reserved. But that was what often happened when someone felt uncomfortable about having given away too much. The next time they met, if she wasn't so busy with Shannon, Abby hoped to make her feel better about it.

"SORRY I'M LATE," Jason Zacharias apologized. "The alarm system at O'Donnell Honda wouldn't disconnect, and I had to replace part of the controller."

"If you'd let me pay you, I'd have a right to complain," Steve assured his friend. He'd been about to call the hospital and see if they could reach Abby, but this was more important.

As Jason opened the door of the electronics van, Steve peered inside. "You've got enough equipment here to support a small army."

"We come prepared." The new vice-president of Randolph and Zacharias Security Services shoved a loaded dolly toward the side door. "You take the receiver, and I'll get the noise generator."

Together, the two men muscled the heavy pieces into the low building that housed Claiborne Carriers. They had the place to themselves since Steve had given his secretary the afternoon off.

"You like working with Cam Randolph?" Steve asked as they started unpacking and setting up the equipment. Cam was Jo O'Malley's husband. When Jason and Noel had returned to Baltimore after their harrowing experiences in Scotland, he'd taken on Jason as a partner.

Jason nodded. "How are Abby and the baby doing?"

"Abby's been out of the hospital for a few weeks, but Shannon won't be released until she gains a few more pounds." He sighed. "It's been rough."

Jason nodded as he adjusted the readout on a digital display. Neither man had much experience confiding domestic worries. Quickly they got back to the security problem—checking for hidden transmitters in Steve's office.

After their initial interview, he'd been pretending to cooperate with McGuire and Driscoll, sending them off on a couple of wild-goose chases to inaccessible places where he "thought" Ollie might be holed up. Then he'd played dumb when they'd come up empty-handed. He knew it was only a stopgap tactic, but it was the best he could do at the moment.

If he'd only had himself to think about, he'd have asked Jason to get him a plane for a secret flight to one of Ollie's real bolt holes so he could ask him what the hell was going on. As things stood, he had to stay here in Baltimore. He couldn't leave Abby while Shannon was still in the hospital. And he'd be even more afraid to leave her alone when the baby came home.

So he'd sent Oliver more than one message via circuitous routes. So far none of them had been answered.

And a couple of days ago the agents had changed their tactics, making a show of stomping off in disgust. He suspected the maneuver was calculated to make him drop his guard, maybe even put through a call to Oliver Gibbs. Instead he'd become more wary.

"How does this stuff work?" Steve asked, gesturing toward the equipment.

"That large case we set up in your office was the noise generator, and this is a radio spectrum analyzer. We'll monitor the full range of frequencies from this display. If McGuire and Driscoll have left any bugs, we'll see a disturbance in the reception."

Jason turned on the equipment, and Steve leaned over his shoulder to get a better view. The program started at the lower frequencies and slowly went up the scale. Steve stared at the hypnotizing pattern that danced across the screen, but instead of noting the frequency modulation, he was remembering the heartbeat charted on the monitor attached to Shannon's little body in the neonatal unit. He felt a hollow place open inside his chest and looked away.

A few minutes later, the regular modulation pattern was broken by random spikes. "Well, well, what have we here?" Jason froze the frame so they could get a closer look.

"A bug?"

"That's my best guess. We'll know for sure when we find it."

They spent the next hour checking under drawers, dismantling lamp fixtures, and inspecting everything from flower pots to wall molding.

"Hey, I think I've found something." Steve gestured to the picture of Abby on his desk. A black disc about the size of a small fingernail was tucked inside a corner of the dismantled frame.

Jason took a magnifying glass from his pocket and studied the foreign object. Before commenting, he dropped it into a shielded case. "Yeah, it's a DM-2485. CIA issue, late eighties. There are some jazzier laser-controlled models on the market today, but this one's pretty durable for short-range pickups. I've even planted a few of these myself."

"So you think McGuire and Driscoll are CIA?" Steve asked as he slid Abby's picture back into the wooden frame and set it up on the desk.

"Maybe. Maybe not. They haven't come up in any of our data bases, but we'll take this baby apart in the lab and run the serial numbers through the computer to see if we can trace it to the Defense Department. We might get lucky, but there's a lot of electronic surveillance stuff on the black market." As he packed up the equipment, Jason dispensed some tips about tightening office security.

"Thanks for coming out," Steve said as he helped reload the van.

"Sure. Glad I could help. We'll let you know what we find out. And if there's anything else you need, just give me a call."

"Will do."

As soon as the van pulled away, Steve kicked a shower of stones from the pebbled border along the blacktop. He'd been right about the covert surveillance, but all it proved was that he was up against a couple of professionals.

ABBY WATCHED STEVE steer the car into a parking space in the Freeman Memorial lot.

In just a few minutes, they were bringing their child home, and Abby was bursting with excitement. But below the exhilaration was a nagging feeling of guilt.

When her husband started to pull the keys from the ignition, she laid her hand over his. "Steve, I'm glad we're both here today."

"Did you think I wasn't going to drive the two of you home from the hospital?"

"I wasn't sure. We didn't talk about it until this morning."

Silently he put the keys in his pocket, but she could see him watching her from the corner of his eye.

"When I woke up, I was so thrilled about bringing Shannon home. The first thing I wanted to do was share that with you. But you were already downstairs making coffee. So I lay in bed thinking about the past few weeks. I haven't shared much with you, have I?'' She swallowed painfully. ''I always tell my patients that it's as important to talk about the rotten stuff as well as the good. But I was so scared... I—I couldn't...I'm sorry.''

Steve moved then, turning and pulling her across the console as he wrapped his arms around her shoulders.

''It wasn't just you. I was doing that, too,'' he said in a gruff voice.

Abby closed her eyes, resting her cheek against his chest, breathing in the familiar scent of his body. His fingers stroked through her hair, and she curled her arms around his neck, swamped by a rush of physical sensations. Her husband was such a physical person. And being married to him had made her that way, too.

She brushed her lips against his cheek. ''I think that part of the problem was that we couldn't make love. But I should have tried not to fall asleep as soon as my head hit the pillow.''

A low, angry sound welled up in his chest. ''No, you were running yourself ragged. You needed your rest. Maybe if I'd shown a little restraint six weeks ago, we wouldn't be in this fix.''

Abby's head jerked up. ''What?''

''I've read those books on your bedside table. Having intercourse can make a woman go into labor. Like you did—the morning after the last time I made love to you.''

Abby felt her heart turn over. ''Oh, Steve. You haven't been thinking all this time that it was your fault, have you? Is that why you've hardly been talking to me?''

He didn't answer.

"The doctor hadn't told us to stop. It wasn't necessary. I wasn't having any problems. And I wasn't due for a couple of months."

"Then why the hell did you have her so early?"

Abby swallowed. "I thought it might have been something I'd done."

Steve swore under his breath. "You've been worried about that . . . I didn't realize . . ."

"I've talked to Dr. Goodman. He doesn't know why it happened. He called it bad luck. I've been trying to make it up to her by doing everything I could. Shannon wasn't at home to wake me up in the middle of the night for feedings, so I'd nap in the afternoon and then come back down here . . ."

"Now it's going to be a lot easier for you. She'll be right in the nursery down the hall from our bedroom."

"Yes." Sighing, Abby turned her face into his neck and closed her eyes, feeling better than she had in weeks.

Slowly, as his hand stroked up and down her arm, the tenor of the embrace changed. When his fingers barely brushed against the side of her breast, warmth and arousal she'd been suppressing for weeks stirred within her.

"Steve, I've missed you."

He turned her in his arms and began to nibble at her lips.

She smiled against his mouth.

"You taste good," he whispered huskily. "Just the way I remember."

"So do you. So very good."

He took her full bottom lip between his teeth and bit gently. At the familiar erotic gesture, a bolt of pleasure shot downward through her body.

She knew he felt her response.

"I thought you didn't want me," he whispered, his lips millimeters from hers.

"If you'd kissed me like that, I would have wanted you."

"I was afraid to start anything."

"So was I."

"God, it's been forever." The kiss deepened, and his hand came up between them to cup her breast through the clingy fabric of her knit top. When his thumb stroked across her hardened nipple, she drew in a sharp little breath. For a moment, she wondered if he'd be turned off by her breasts when he saw them. They were heavy with milk, and the nipples were large and dark. Then she stopped thinking about anything besides the wonderful sensations her husband was creating with his hands and lips.

When they finally broke the contact, Abby was breathing hard—and the blood was pounding through her veins. She flattened her palm against Steve's chest, feeling the wild beating of his heart.

"When can we . . . ?" he asked, his voice rough with urgency.

"I've got an appointment with Dr. Goodman tomorrow."

"So tonight I guess we're going to have to improvise."

Abby giggled, her spirit lighter than spun sugar. "Yeah."

A car gunned its engine, and she glanced up, startled. Then she turned her head and smoothed her hair. For a while she'd forgotten everything except Steve. However, the two of them *were* sitting in a public parking lot in broad daylight making out like a pair of teenagers on a deserted lovers' lane.

"I guess I wasn't thinking about where we were," Steve muttered, echoing her thoughts.

"Mmm."

"Abby." His tone had turned serious.

"What?"

"I was worried about Shannon, too."

"I know."

"She was so small. And there were all those tubes and wires and monitors. I was afraid she'd break—or I'd mess up some of the connections—if I tried to pick her up."

"I felt that way, too, the first time I held her."

Steve's eyes had turned the dark stormy blue that signaled strong emotions. "I'm going to try to be a good father to her. Not like my dad."

"I've known that all along."

He looked at his watch. "The nursing staff is probably wondering where we are."

After stepping out onto the sidewalk, Steve reached into the back seat for the rectangular diaper bag Abby had packed several days earlier. Inside, along with the usual baby supplies, was a tiny green dress with pink rosebuds that Shannon was going to wear on the trip home.

Slinging the plastic strap over his shoulder as if he were thoroughly accustomed to carrying a diaper bag, Steve came around to Abby's side of the car. When they started up the sidewalk toward the main entrance, he reached for her hand.

She gave his fingers an encouraging squeeze. When he squeezed back, she smiled.

"Thanks for being here."

"Abby, I'm trying—"

"I know."

"We'll get Shannon settled in her room. Then I'll pick up some takeout so you don't have to worry about fixing dinner."

"Thanks." Her grip tightened on his hand. "Are you going to tell me what else has been bothering you?"

"Stuff at work."

"Can I help?"

He shook his head. "I'm trying to get it cleared up."

They had reached the hospital entrance. Steve pulled open the glass door, and they stepped into the cool, quiet interior.

The neonatology ward was on the second floor. As soon as the elevator opened, Abby knew something unusual was going on.

Several staffers milled around the nursing station. A security guard leaned over the desk, talking rapidly into the telephone. And a woman from the administrative staff was striding down the hall toward the nursery.

The head nurse, Mrs. Daly, a tiny woman with iron-gray hair, came rushing toward the elevator. "Dr. Franklin, Mr. Claiborne. We've been trying to get you on the phone. You weren't by any chance here earlier, were you?"

"No. What's wrong?" Abby asked, feeling her mouth go dry even as she got the words out. "Is—is something wrong with Shannon?"

The woman's expression knocked the air from Abby's lungs. Without waiting for an explanation, she began to run down the hall toward the nursery.

"Wait," someone called after her.

She heard something bulky thunk to the floor behind her, but she didn't break her stride. Heavy footsteps kept pace with her. Palming the latch and throwing open the door, she skidded to a stop in front of the isolette where Shannon had been sleeping yesterday evening.

It was empty.

Chapter Three

Leaning over the little crib, Abby stared down at the smooth, white mattress. If she looked closely, she could see the indentation where a tiny body had lain.

A second later, Steve came up behind her, his hands gripping her arms. Mrs. Daly, puffing hard, skidded to a stop, almost bumping into him.

"Is she...s-sick...? What...?" Abby choked out, her fingers gripping the curved plastic side of the bed. "Where have you taken her?"

"She's not sick. At least, we don't think so—"

Steve whirled to face the nurse. "Then what the hell's going on?"

Mrs. Daly's arms dropped heavily to her sides. "Your daughter has disappeared."

"But that's impossible!" Abby gasped. She didn't realize her knees had buckled until she felt Steve's hands under her elbows, supporting her weight.

"Sweetheart, let go of the crib. You've got to sit down." His fingers tried to loosen hers. As if she'd just discovered that her hands still worked, she suddenly let go.

Steve steered her toward a chair, and she sank down heavily. Then he rounded on the nurse. "Explain."

"The only thing I know is that Shannon Claiborne is missing. We were going to get her ready for you, but she wasn't in her bed."

"Missing! What the hell kind of security do you have around this place?" Steve roared.

Mrs. Daly took a step back. "We're checking to see if another department has her, for tests or a procedure."

"What tests?" Steve continued to grill the woman.

"Well, nothing was ordered by Dr. Wilmer. But sometimes there are mix-ups. We're hoping—"

Steve swore vehemently. "You're telling me you can't find our daughter? You don't even know whether she's in the hospital?"

Abby listened in growing horror. Wrapping her arms around herself, she tried to keep her body from shaking. Shannon wasn't here. They didn't know where she was.

"Have you called the police?" Steve asked.

"No, we—"

"Do it!"

The woman bounded off like a donkey that had been swatted on the rump. The commotion had awakened several tiny babies, who began to cry. Abby stared at the closest one as if she'd just come out of a drugged sleep. Mrs. Daly had said there was a mix-up. Maybe—

Scrambling out of her chair, she peered down at the red-faced infant. Not Shannon. Heart beating, hoping against hope, Abby checked the other residents of the nursery. But her daughter wasn't in one of the little beds.

She tried to bite back a cry of anguish. It came out as a muffled sob. Steve was instantly at her side, taking her elbow. "Come on. Let's get out of here."

"No!"

He turned her toward him, wrapping his arms protectively around her quivering body. She felt him trembling, too. For a moment neither of them moved away from the crib. Then he bent and spoke very gently against her hair. "I don't mean out of the hospital. Just down the hall."

"Okay." Abby let him steer her from the nursery.

People still milled around the nurses' station, but they all swung in their direction as Abby and Steve came slowly down the hall. Abby turned her head away, hoping that no one was going to rush up and tell her how sorry they were. If they did, she would come undone.

Her eyes focused on the diaper bag still lying on the floor near the wall where Steve had dropped it. Tightening his hold on her arm, he quickly ushered her into the waiting room. Moments later Mrs. Daly joined them.

"You called the police?" Steve asked.

"Yes."

"While we're waiting for them, tell me how someone could come into the nursery and take a baby."

"Mr. Claiborne, our security is very strict. Every visitor to the floor passes through a security check, and we have sign-in sheets for every one of our paid employees and volunteers."

A staff physician, Dr. Scott, came in. "I've just heard about what happened, and I know the two of you are upset—"

"You're damn right," Steve grated.

Abby glanced at her husband's rigid face, knowing he was as close to the edge as she was herself. But he was handling it differently—by channeling his fear into anger toward the hospital staff.

The physician continued to talk to Steve, but Abby wasn't listening to the conversation. She was trying to keep her own terror under control as she thought about Shannon. Oh, God, her daughter was still so tiny. Was she frightened? Who had her? Did they know she'd been born prematurely, that she still needed special care? Did they even know how to support her head when they picked her up?

"Why did you take my baby?" she whispered.

"Do you have any idea who that might be?" a new voice questioned.

Everyone in the room turned to face the compact, muscular man who had asked the question. "Will Angel, Detective, Baltimore Police Department." He flipped open his wallet, displaying a badge.

"Thank God," Abby breathed. Finally someone was going to do something. "You've got to find Shannon."

"You're Mrs. Claiborne?"

"Yes. I mean, I—I use my maiden name, Dr. Franklin." She closed her eyes, trying to remember the first question he'd asked. "No, I—I...don't know who could do something like this." Her voice broke on the last words, and she clamped her mouth shut. Steve came down beside her, kneeling on the floor as he gripped her hand.

"You're Mr. Claiborne?" Angel asked.

"Yeah."

"Do *you* have any idea who might have taken your child from the hospital?"

Abby felt Steve's body stiffen, and her head swung questioningly toward him. But he only shrugged.

The detective turned to Mrs. Daly. "You're in charge of this ward?"

"Yes."

"Has anyone suspicious been hanging around the nursery?"

She repeated the security information she'd given Abby and Steve.

"Do you have a picture of the baby?" Angel asked Abby.

"Yes. I've been taking them all along." Looking around for her pocketbook, she was astonished to find the strap still slung over her arm. Fumbling inside, she drew out the packet of photographs she'd been showing off. There was even one a nurse had taken of her, Steve, and Shannon together on one of his rare visits to the hospital.

"Pick the one that looks most like her, and we'll get it out right away with our missing person's bulletin."

As Abby began to shuffle through the snapshots, her vision blurred. In one picture, Shannon was reaching out a hand toward her from the isolette. "You do it," Abby whispered to Steve.

A regretful look flashed across his face, and he shook his head. "You know her better than I do."

Abby struggled to complete the task. "These three are the best," she finally said to Angel. Swallowing hard, she tucked the packet back into her purse.

"We can get her description and vital statistics from the nursing staff."

The detective and Mrs. Daly left the room. Steve got up, paced to the window and turned back toward Abby. She thought he was about to say something, but he closed his mouth again.

Abby drew up her legs and rested her chin on her knees. Her breasts hurt where they pressed against her thighs, but she didn't change position. She needed to hold herself together, needed to hold the contents of her stomach inside her body.

Steve stood staring out the window as if he were hoping someone would come back across the parking lot with Shannon wrapped securely in a receiving blanket. But that wasn't very likely.

"What if someone's holding her for ransom?" Abby asked.

At the sound of her voice, he whirled toward her. "Because they know both the Franklins and the Claibornes are wealthy?"

"Yes."

"I wasn't thinking about anything like that." Strangely, Steve sounded almost relieved as he started toward the door.

"Where are you going?"

"To talk to Angel. Somebody ought to be stationed at our house in case there's a call or a note."

"Wait!"

He turned back toward Abby.

"Not the police," she said. "Kidnappers might not want the authorities involved. See if Jo will do it. And ask her not to talk to anyone."

Steve knelt beside her again. "Are you going to be okay if I leave?"

"No. I'm not going to be any better until we get her back."

"Abby, I know how you—" He stopped. "No. I guess I don't know how you feel. But I'm frightened. And angry." He stopped again.

She reached for his hand and squeezed it. "I understand."

"I'll go call Jo."

When the door closed behind Steve, Abby felt alone and defenseless. Would anyone hear her if she started to scream or pound the wall? Instead she gripped her legs more tightly.

"Just don't hurt her," she whispered. "Don't hurt my baby, and I'll pay you anything you want. Just give her back to me."

Yet it might not be that simple. It might not be a matter of money at all.

Her breath grew shallow as she thought over various cases described in psychology journals and the newspapers. Babies were sometimes stolen by lonely women who wanted someone to love. Women who didn't have or couldn't bear their own children.

Abby's heart skipped a beat. Shannon had been here for six weeks. What if she'd been stolen by someone who'd come to love her while they took care of her?

Leaping off the sofa, she dashed into the hall. Angel was conferring with the woman from the administrative offices and Dr. Scott, who looked as if he'd rather be in the middle of a heart and lung transplant operation.

The detective glanced in her direction, and she caught an expression on his face that she didn't like. He was thinking of her as the hysterical mother, someone who would only get in the way of the investigation. She couldn't let him see how broken up she was inside.

"Do you have the records of everyone who's been working in the nursery over the past six weeks?" she asked the administrative staffer in a voice that sounded surprisingly steady to her own ears.

"They're on the way up."

While they waited, Angel explained that Shannon's photograph and description were already being circulated around the city. There wasn't anything more concrete he could tell her, so he went off to find out which employees and volunteers had been on duty that afternoon.

Bone-tired and dispirited, Abby dropped onto the couch and glanced down the hall. Where was Steve? Couldn't he reach Jo? Was he trying to get another one of their friends to go out to the house?

She was sitting with her eyes closed when the sound of her name made her jump.

"Sorry." It was Mrs. Daly.

"Do you have the files?"

"Yes."

Mrs. Daly, Angel, and Abby repaired to the conference room at the end of the corridor.

"It's less likely to be a long-time employee, so separate the files into two stacks," the detective instructed Mrs. Daly. "Those who have been with the hospital for several years, and those who joined the staff shortly before or right after Dr. Franklin's baby arrived in the nursery."

Abby watched tensely as the woman went through the pile. She didn't even see the uniformed officer standing in the doorway until he started to speak.

"We've questioned the two volunteers who were supposed to be on duty. Mrs. Lewis went straight from the hospital to choir practice. Her husband picked her up. The other lady, Mrs. Brandford, wasn't here today."

"But we have her signature," Angel retorted, shuffling through the stack of cards in front of him and holding one up. "It's right here."

"She said she got a call not to come in, so she went to visit her daughter in Arbutus. Arrived there at 10:00 a.m. They went to lunch and shopping at Security Mall."

Mrs. Daly reached for the card. "That's her name. She signed in at 2:15 p.m. But I don't recall seeing her on the floor. We were shorthanded, so I was glad when

I spotted Mrs. Hamadi." She looked perplexed. "Come to think of it, I only caught a quick glance at her from the back—a woman in long, baggy pants with a scarf over her head."

She looked at Abby for confirmation. "That's the way she dresses, isn't it?"

"Yes. She always has her hair covered. And she wears those big culottes."

"Did you see her leave?" the detective interjected.

"I'm not sure how long she was here. As I said, I only had a glimpse of her back. She was walking toward the stairs."

"The stairs. Not the elevator?" Angel clarified.

"The elevators are right across from the nursing station. She was heading down the hall."

Abby felt a shiver go through her body. Mrs. Hamadi. A sad, lonely woman who'd borne and lost three premature infants. A woman who'd taken a special interest in Shannon. A woman who'd confided her sorrow to Abby and then avoided her.

"How long has she worked here?" Angel asked.

"She's our newest volunteer." Mrs. Daly shuffled through the folders and opened one. "She completed the training program on August 14 and did her first shift on August 15."

"Ten days after Shannon was born!" Abby breathed.

"STEVE! Where were you?"

"Jo was out on a case. I got Erin Morgan." He peered anxiously into Abby's face. "Did something happen?"

"There's this woman, a volunteer in the nursery. Mrs. Hamadi." Abby began to pour out the story. "One night in the hospital we got to talking. I told her

how worried I was, and she told me about losing her
own premature babies. Then she started avoiding me.
She kept looking at Shannon as if she wanted her. But
I didn't think..."

"Of course not."

"The police are on their way to her apartment now."

Steve sat down beside Abby, and she slid close to
him, laying her head on his shoulder.

"Oh, God, let her be there," she whispered.

Steve squeezed her fingers. Neither of them spoke.

This is what a waiting room in hell is like, Abby
thought. The seconds dragged by. Finally, footsteps
echoed in the hall, and moments later Angel appeared
in the doorway. When Abby saw the stark expression
on the detective's face, she felt her body go cold.
"What's happened? What's happened to Shannon?"

"I'm sorry, but we still don't know. The address
Mrs. Hamadi gave on her volunteer application was
faked. No one there has heard of her."

Abby started to bury her face in her hands but
stopped herself.

"I know you're disappointed," Angel said. "But
there are other ways to trace the woman."

"Disappointed" hardly described her feeling.
"Devastated" came closer.

One of the uniformed officers came into the room
and handed Angel a sheet of paper, which the detective scanned quickly. When he looked up, his expression was grimmer than before. "The woman's folder
disappeared from the training department—if it ever
existed."

Abby nodded numbly.

"Do you think you could help a police artist produce a sketch of her?"

"Yes." She sat up straighter, grateful for the chance to do something. "Her face was unusual, and I'll never forget her eyes."

"Good. I'll get someone down here within twenty minutes." As Angel turned to leave the room, she called him back.

"Wait! It's almost five. The evening news is on in an hour. Do you think we could contact one of the local TV stations and ask if they'd let me and Steve make a broadcast? We could ask if anyone has seen Shannon, and also make a...a...plea for the kidnapper to bring her back."

Angel looked thoughtful. "Let's wait until the late news, just in case something develops in the meantime. Also, it will give you some time to think about exactly what to say, and for the police artist to produce a picture that the camera can show."

Abby nodded eagerly. Then she turned to Steve. "What do you think?"

"I think I'm willing to try anything that will get our daughter back."

Chapter Four

Back home in the pink and green nursery with its cute baby animal wallpaper, Abby stood beside the empty crib, stroking her fingers along the top of the railing like a blind woman trying to memorize a hard, un-yielding shape. And in truth, she could barely see through the film of tears that blurred her vision. Somehow in the hospital and at the TV studio she'd held herself together. Here, however, she hadn't been able to keep back the tears of loss and pain. For weeks she'd imagined carrying Shannon into the house, up the stairs, and into this room that she'd lovingly deco-rated for her child. Now she secretly wondered if she ever would.

She wiped her hands across her cheeks and stood straighter. "I'll get you back," she whispered fiercely into the empty room. "I will. You're in Baltimore. In the same city. Maybe not in the apartment where Mrs. Hamadi claimed she was living, but somewhere close by."

She wanted to hate Mrs. Hamadi. She couldn't. The woman had picked Shannon because she loved her. And she'd take good care of her, just the way she'd learned in the hospital. At least that was something. At least she knew Mrs. Hamadi had been trained to care for Shannon.

Abby squeezed her eyes shut as she pictured Mrs. Hamadi holding Shannon and stroking a hand gently across her back.

"You don't exist in a vacuum," Abby continued, this time whispering her words to the woman instead of her daughter. "Somebody will recognize your picture. Somebody will tell me where you're really living."

"Sweetheart?" Abby wiped her eyes again.

Steve crossed the room and circled her shoulders with his arm. "I heard you talking."

"To Shannon. And Mrs. Hamadi. I'm turning into a regular mental case."

"No."

"I know it's stupid, but I can't help it. It makes me feel . . . connected."

Steve nodded. "There's nothing wrong with that, if it helps you." He tugged gently on her shoulder. "We're both exhausted. Come lie down."

"I can't."

"Making yourself sick isn't going to do Shannon any good."

Abby couldn't fight his logic. In fact, after the longest twelve hours of her life, she couldn't fight much of anything. Wearily she allowed Steve to lead her down the hall to their bedroom.

Instead of getting undressed, she flopped down on top of the spread. If Detective Angel called to say he'd found Shannon, she wanted to be able to go to her immediately.

STEVE STRETCHED OUT beside his wife. The day Shannon had been born, he'd wanted to lie down beside Abby and take her in his arms, to shield her and protect her and show her how precious she was to him. Now he rolled to his side and pulled her close. She pressed her face against his neck, and he felt her slender body tremble in his embrace.

"We'll get our baby back," he murmured. He didn't know if it was true. He only knew his wife needed to hold on to that hope. The way she was holding on to him.

He was pretty sure that if he said anything else, his voice would break. So he simply clung to Abby, fighting to get control of himself. In the semidarkness, they lay that way for several minutes.

Yet there were things he needed to tell her, things he'd kept to himself because he didn't want to worry her. Since this afternoon, he'd realized how grave a mistake he'd made. But it wasn't just a matter of not confiding in her. It was also a matter of not taking action.

Abby must have sensed the unspoken words that were clogging his throat. "What?" she questioned softly.

"I can tell how bad this is for you," he said in a low voice.

"It's bad for you, too. You just deal with it differently."

"Yeah." He sucked in a sharp breath and let it out in a rush. "Abby, I'm sorry."

"It's not your fault."

The confession he'd dreaded tumbled from his lips. "Maybe it is."

"What?" She put enough distance between them so that she could look at him. "What do you mean? How could it be your fault?"

He wanted to twist away from her, but he didn't. "Remember how you kept asking me what was wrong, what was bothering me—besides Shannon being born early, I mean?''

Abby nodded.

"And remember when you went into labor, and Jan couldn't find me?'' He swallowed. "I didn't leave a number where I could be reached because I was in a motel room near BWI airport being interrogated by two government agents.''

"Interrogated?'' Abby sat up.

He did, too. "Yeah. Since then, they've been back to question me half a dozen times. I'm pretty sure they work for the CIA.''

"What does that have to do with Mrs. Hamadi—and Shannon?'' Reaching for the switch, Abby turned on the reading light hanging over their bed. They both blinked in the sudden brightness.

He ran his fingers through his hair. "The CIA is desperate to contact Oliver Gibbs.''

"Your old partner?''

"Yeah.'' He went on to describe the sessions he'd had with the agents over the past few weeks and the monitoring device he'd discovered in his office.

"Why didn't you tell me?'' Abby demanded when he'd finally run out of explanations.

"You had enough to worry about. I thought this was something I could handle by myself.''

Her brow wrinkled. "I don't understand what the CIA's looking for Oliver has to do with our baby,'' she said.

"One of the agents threatened me by pointing out that I had a wife—and child—now. He said I'd better worry about them if I wasn't planning to play ball.''

"Steve, the CIA doesn't kidnap the babies of American citizens to try to force them to reveal information. It doesn't carry out *any* operations inside the U.S. at all. That's illegal.''

''So was Watergate. But maybe we're not dealing with the CIA. Maybe somebody else is looking for Oliver and pretending they work for the government.''

Abby shook her head. ''We know who took Shannon. A sad, lonely woman who wanted a baby of her own.''

''Do we?''

''Mrs. Hamadi was in the hospital this afternoon, but she signed in with someone else's name. She was seen hurrying toward the stairs. She falsified all of her records.''

''That doesn't disprove anything I've just said! She could have been working for somebody else.''

''Did you share your hypothesis with Angel?''

''No. The agents warned me to keep the investigation confidential. I don't know whether or not ratting on them would make things worse, and I'm not about to put it to the test.''

He couldn't stand the look of anguish on her face. The only consolation he could give her was to drag her into his arms again. She clung to him, her shoulders shaking and her breath uneven, and he knew she was fighting not to break into a million pieces. God, he wasn't helping her. He was making things worse.

''Steve, please—''

The shattered tone in her voice tore through him.''Abby, sweetheart. Everything's going to be all right. It's going to be all right.'' He said it over and over—for himself as much as her. He wondered if she believed him.

''Help me get her back.''

''I will. I will.'' He pressed her close for a moment longer, then gently eased away from her. Still unable to

face the pain in her eyes, he strode to his dresser and
began to pull open drawers.

"What . . . what are you doing?"

"The only thing I can. I'm going to find Ollie Gibbs
and shake the truth out of him."

She stared at him as if she were trying to figure out
whether she'd heard him right.

"What?"

"Sweetheart, I've sent messages to Ollie, but I
haven't gotten any word back. The only way I can find
out what's going on is to see for myself. So I'm using
one of Jason Zacharias's contacts. He's lined me up a
small jet at Dulles Airport. All I have to do is make
sure I'm not being followed when I leave here—or lose
the tail. And I still remember enough from the old days
to do that."

"So you're telling me you don't think Shannon is in
Baltimore."

"Not necessarily. I don't know where she is!"

"And what should I tell Angel? That my husband's
gone off on a wild-goose chase?"

"Tell him the truth—if you think he'll keep it confidential. It might help with his investigation."

"Where is Oliver?"

He stopped in the act of pulling a shirt out of the
drawer. "One of two places. I'll check the most likely
one—and then the other."

"You mean somewhere in India? That's like saying
somewhere in Australia."

"Sweetheart, I can't be any more specific."

"Why not?"

"You can't give out information you don't have."

He saw her fingers clutching at the bedspread.

"Are you telling me I can't contact you while you're
gone?"

"God, Abby, I'm sorry. It's safer that way, for both you and Shannon. I'll check in with you in a couple of days."

"Listen to me," she said, her voice rising in frustration. "Hamadi is a Muslim name. Muslims aren't that prominent in India. What could this have to do with Oliver?"

Steve sighed. "He transports cargo to lots of places outside India. Pakistan, for example. It's full of Muslims. Besides, you don't think Hamadi is her real name, do you?"

He could see there was no way she was going to believe him. Not, and keep functioning rationally. She was clinging to the hope that her daughter had been stolen by a lonely woman who would love her and take care of her. But if what he was saying were true, then Shannon could be anywhere. Literally anywhere in the world. And God knew what kind of people had her.

He understood why Abby simply couldn't allow herself to think in those terms. But one of them had to do it.

"Maybe Angel will find her." He crossed the room and gave her one last, fierce hug.

She held on to him as if her arms around his body could keep him from leaving, but she didn't continue the argument. She knew him too well. When he said he was going to do something, he did it.

Only this time, she probably thought he was off his rocker. For all he knew, she was right. But he couldn't keep repeating the mistakes he'd made over the past few weeks. If Ollie had something to do with this and he didn't find out, he'd never forgive himself.

"You work on it from this end. I'll find out how Ollie fits into it. That way we'll double our chances."

He knew she didn't agree with him. But that was the best he could do before he forced himself to walk away from her.

THE NEXT forty-eight hours were the longest of Abby's life. Steve was gone. Shannon was still missing. Fear was a gnawing tiger in her chest that grew fiercer with every passing hour. She was bone weary, but she couldn't sleep.

Yet she kept going. Somehow, she didn't allow herself to stop functioning.

Steve had let her down. No. She shouldn't think about it that way. He'd left Baltimore because he was doing what he thought was right. And if he couldn't be here to help her, she had to rely on her own strength.

Dozens of tips had flooded in to the police after their late-night television appeal, which had been rebroadcast on all the local channels on the noon news. Angel was doing what he could, but it took time and manpower to sort the crank calls from the real possibilities. The crew at 43 Light Street had pooled their skills and resources to help with the search. Jo and Cam were checking out leads. Noel and Laura were trying to track Mrs. Hamadi through immigration records. Erin Morgan, Sabrina's former employee, was also in the thick of things. Recently appointed regional manager of Birth Data, Inc., a search service for adoptees trying to locate their birth parents, she had turned her fourth-floor office into a clearinghouse for information. She was also sifting through adoption requests on the theory that the kidnapper might have tried to get a baby legally before she'd snatched Shannon.

The early leads they'd gotten had not panned out. Then the police received a call from the manager at the Greenway Apartments off Putty Hill Road. One of his

tenants matched the woman's description—even down
to the pierced nose shown in the police drawing. And
a neighbor had complained of a baby crying the night
before. That information was enough for the police to
request a search warrant and rush it through the
courthouse procedure.

By six that evening, Abby was riding with Detective
Angel toward the apartment complex. He'd had to pull
some strings to get her approved; technically, she was
a psychologist assigned to the case. Allowing her to
come along was a tribute to the fortitude she'd worked
so hard to project—and to the working relationship
they'd developed.

Please, God. Let this be the one. Abby laced stiff
fingers together in her lap as she watched the run-down
commercial properties along the Jones Falls Express-
way fade into more residential areas. As the police car
turned up Northern Parkway, she glanced gratefully at
Angel. When she'd first met him at the hospital, she'd
thought he was cold. Over the past two days, she'd
come to understand that he needed to stay detached,
just the way she had to with her patients. In a way, it
was a role reversal for her. She was the needy client,
and he was the competent professional. He was also a
man putting in twenty hours a day trying to find
Shannon.

He slowed down as they turned onto Putty Hill
Road. "The place is in the next block on the left."

The apartments were garden-style, mid-sixties vin-
tage. They found Hal Stuwarski, the manager, pacing
nervously in the parking lot outside the office. He was
a small, stringy man with curly red hair.

"Mr. Stuwarski, this is Dr. Franklin, and I'm Will
Angel with the Baltimore City police."

"What took you so long?"

"We had to get a search warrant."

"Yeah, I guess I wasn't thinking about all that legal stuff."

Abby wished he'd stayed inside and pretended that this were just a normal day. But it was too late to tell him that now.

"I'll need your master key to the apartment," Angel said.

"Sure thing." The manager detached a key from the dozen or so that hung from a ring on his workman's belt. "I'll take you over to her place."

Outside, another police car had pulled into the parking lot. Angel motioned for the two uniformed officers to join them.

He stationed one guard by the door to the unit and then turned to Abby. "I'll be out again as soon as I can."

"I'm going in with you."

"I can't put a civilian in jeopardy. You know you've got to wait here."

"Will, you're supposed to be relying on my professional judgment. Let me make an appeal to the woman. I may be able to talk her into letting Shannon go."

Angel seemed to realize that it was either give in or handcuff her to the railing. "Okay. But stay in the back and do what I tell you."

The apartment was on the third floor. As Abby followed the men up the stairs, the strong smell of garlic, onions and olive oil wafted down. By the time they'd reached the third-floor landing, the stale odor was making Abby nauseated.

Holding her breath, she watched Angel rap loudly on the door.

"Police. Open up, please."

No answer.

After trying again with the same result, he motioned Abby to stand back and used the master key to unlock the door. Both men drew their service revolvers.

"No, no guns!" Abby choked out. "Shannon might get hurt."

Angel gave her a long look and then nodded to the officer. They reholstered their weapons before moving cautiously into the living room. Disobeying orders, Abby inched to the doorway, her ears straining for the sound of her baby's cry. But she heard nothing. Heart pounding, she stepped across the threshold. The room was as bare as a desert nomad's abandoned campsite. A faded Indian rug on the floor with a hibachi grill in the center were the only furnishings. And the onion-garlic smell lingered in the air.

"Mrs. Hamadi?" Abby called frantically. There was no answer.

"The place is empty," Angel confirmed as he emerged from the bedroom.

"There's still food in the refrigerator, and it looks like the hibachi was used this morning," the uniformed officer reported. "Smells like it, too. I think we just missed her."

Disappointment swept over Abby like a flash flood. The only way she stayed on her feet was to slump back against the wall. She'd been so psyched up to confront the woman who had taken Shannon, so sure she could convince her to give her child back. But now...

Around her, the men were starting a more thorough search. Angel was in the kitchen. The other man was in the bedroom. Abby pushed herself erect and went to check out the bathroom.

The counter and medicine cabinet were empty. So was the trash can—as if the apartment had been swept clean of evidence. But as she put it back in the corner, her eyes spotted a little ball of fuzz on the floor. She picked it up. No. It wasn't fuzz, it was fine black hair. Just like from Shannon's little brush! Something seemed to break apart in her chest as she smoothed the silky strands between her fingers.

"Shannon *was* here!" Abby clasped the evidence in her fist as she dashed back into the living room.

"Hmm, looks like baby hair. We'll send this to the lab," Angel said as he got out a small plastic bag.

"I know Shannon was here," Abby insisted.

"You may be right. We'll question the people in the neighborhood. If we're lucky, somebody saw the two of them leave."

ABBY KEPT UP a show of optimism until she locked the door behind Detective Angel.

This was the only occasion since the kidnapping when the house had been empty. Every other time she'd gone out, she'd asked a friend to stay by the phone, in case they received a ransom message. But she'd been so sure she would find Shannon that she hadn't made the usual arrangements.

Now she was thankful she was alone. Pretending to be strong in front of her friends took too much energy.

As soon as no one could see her, her whole posture changed. Head down and shoulders hunched, she started slowly for the stairs. Her legs felt as if someone had strapped ten-pound exercise weights to her ankles, and she had to grip the banister to pull herself along. What was the use of going up, anyway? she wondered. There wasn't a chance of getting any sleep when she reached her bedroom. But if she stayed downstairs she'd feel as if she should eat something, and she couldn't face food, either. Probably she should let Jo or Noel know she was home. But conversation was also beyond her. In the end, she decided a darkened bedroom was her best option.

As she plodded down the long, empty corridor, she was struck with a vague sensation that something was wrong. Stopping in her tracks, she dragged in a lungful of air. Her house smelled a little like Mrs. Hamadi's apartment.

Like olive oil and garlic.

Knowing that her senses were playing tricks on her, she started walking again. But the vague odor seemed to grow stronger.

After switching on the light, she turned toward the bed and froze. In the middle of the spread, where she couldn't possibly miss it, was a square envelope.

Abby's heart leapt. Steve. It was from Steve! He'd come home, found her gone, and left some vital information.

Flying across the room, she snatched up the envelope. It was heavy and rigid, like the kind that contained a wedding invitation or a birth announcement. And it smelled funny.

With shaky hands, she lifted it to her nose and sniffed. Olive oil and garlic.

Quickly she slit the flap and pulled out a folded sheet of paper—and a picture of a baby lying on a striped blanket.

Shannon! And not one of the pictures she'd taken. A new one.

Against all odds, had Steve somehow found their child? Was this the proof? As her eyes scanned the first line of type, the photograph fluttered silently to the carpet.

Mrs. Claiborne,
You must quickly contact your husband if you ever want to see your daughter alive again.

Chapter Five

Abby didn't know her knees had given way until she found herself sitting on the edge of the bed, the paper grasped in her rigid fingers. Her gaze flickered to the signature at the bottom of the page.

"Amarjit Singh. For the Indian Liberation Army."

In a panic, Abby realized she was no longer holding the picture that had come with the note. Frantically, she began to search over the bed and then the floor. Finally she found the photograph lying beside her right foot.

Leaning over, she snatched it up, cradling it protectively in her hand as she studied her daughter's tiny face, her raised arms and legs. Shannon was all right. She was still all right.

Then she forced herself to read the rest of the message. The language was stilted, but the meaning was unmistakable.

Medical examination determines Shannon Claiborne can survive a lengthy journey. By the time you are receiving this communication, your daughter will be out of the U.S. of A. She is being held by the ILA. We will return her to you in exchange for the shipment of materials stolen from us by your husband's partner, Oliver Gibbs. If the transaction is failing to materialize within ten days, the little girl's life is forfeit. She will also be killed if you attempt to convey this information to the CIA—or fail to disconnect your dealings with the local police. More instructions for you and Steve Claiborne are following.

Shivering violently, Abby read the words again. Then, raising her head, she looked around the room. Someone had broken into her home while she'd been off with Angel. Someone had come upstairs, right into her bedroom, and left this terrible threat.

Were they still here, waiting to see what she would do?

She sat very still, listening, but the house was as quiet as a tomb. All she could hear was the roaring of blood in her own ears. And, really, it made no sense that whoever had left the note would still be lurking around. They didn't want to confront her face-to-face. They wanted something from Steve—in exchange for Shannon.

The words of the message sank in more deeply, and Abby felt as if every molecule of air had been siphoned from the room. Gasping for breath, she got up and staggered to the door. My God, Steve had been right all along, and she hadn't believed him.

Afraid that she was going to faint, she slid down to the floor and lowered her head between her legs until the feeling of dizziness passed.

Then she cautiously got up and grabbed for the phone. As she started to dial, she remembered that the police had put a tap on the line. She considered what she was going to say before calling Jason Zacharias.

Noel answered. "Abby! Has something happened? Is there any word on Shannon?"

She swallowed a little gulp. "I thought I wouldn't mind staying here alone, but I'm starting to feel nervous with Steve gone. Could you and Jason come over?"

"Of course. We'll be there as soon as we can."

"Thanks."

Abby sat and waited, fighting her panic by forcing herself to study the oddly worded note for clues. It was written by someone who didn't speak English very well. Or someone who was pretending that they didn't.

She knew they'd already lied about one thing. Shannon had not been out of the country when this message had been delivered. Mrs. Hamadi had been at the Greenway Apartments shortly before the police arrived, and Shannon had been there with her.

When the doorbell rang, Abby scrambled off the bed and headed for the front hall. Looking through the side window, she breathed a sigh of relief when she saw both Jason and Noel standing on the porch.

After stepping inside, Noel gave her a fierce hug. Jason patted her awkwardly on the arm.

"Something happened. What?" he asked as soon as the door closed.

Abby regarded him quizzically. In many ways, he was like her husband. They were both tough, and smart, and had learned about life the hard way. But Jason was more controlled, less impulsive than Steve. And he wasn't a man who let his private thoughts show—unless he wanted his views known. "How did you know something happened?" she asked him.

"You've let your friends help you look for Shannon. You haven't asked for help getting through the night."

Abby nodded tightly. "Come into the den. I want to show you something."

When the couple was seated on the couch, Abby handed over the message.

"Oh, Abby—" Noel breathed. "I'm so sorry."

"Jason, did Steve tell you where he was going?" she asked.

"Borneo."

Borneo? She couldn't even place the country on a map. If it was a country. "Are you sure? How do you know?"

"He had to log a flight plan."

"That's right."

"But I've got more than his destination. He gave me a sealed note and told me not to open it unless there was an emergency." Jason pulled a business-size envelope from an inside jacket pocket.

Abby stared at it. "He gave that to you, not me," she whispered.

"No one was going to try to pry the information out of me," Jason replied evenly, "because nobody realized I had it."

Abby nodded, only somewhat mollified. "I guess you'd better open it."

"He may have left it with me for safekeeping, but it's really for you," Jason said gruffly, handing it over.

Abby moved to the couch between her friends. Then, with shaky fingers, she slit the seal. Inside was a set of dates, contact points, and contingency plans.

"It says Steve was going to call you if he found Oliver at the first destination," Jason muttered as he looked from the paper to the date window on his watch. "This is the fifteenth. Have you heard from him?"

"No." Abby ran her eyes down the page. "Then he's going on to New Delhi. Unless his plans have changed," she added in a voice that rose in desperation.

Noel put an arm around her shoulder. "Oh, honey. We'll figure it out."

Abby looked at Jason. "Can you arrange a flight for me—the way you did for Steve?"

"You're not going there alone!" Noel objected.

"I have to. I have to help him get Shannon back. I was so sure I had it all figured out, that Shannon was taken by a woman who was obsessed with having a baby of her own. But it was only what I wanted to believe. Steve tried to tell me the kidnapping was tied up with Oliver. I wouldn't listen to him."

"You were acting on the best information you had," Noel said, trying to comfort her.

"I wasn't acting on information! I was acting on emotion." Abby took a deep breath and let it out slowly. "I still think it was Mrs. Hamadi. But she must have been working for this group called the Indian Liberation Army." Her voice grew shaky, and she stopped abruptly. She'd gone from one firmly held conviction to another in the space of a few minutes, and the transition left her breathless. If she were one of her own patients, she'd probably suggest a good, stiff dose of Valium. But she didn't have that luxury. She needed to think. And act.

"The ILA said they're going to contact you with further instructions," Noel said softly.

"And then what? I can't tell them where Oliver is." Abby pressed her knuckles against her lips, then she raise her eyes to her friend. "Don't you understand? I can't just sit here waiting, not when I've wasted all this time. But you could stay at my house in case they call. Or if you can't do it, someone else."

"I'll do it," Noel reassured her. "Erin and I can work in shifts. But you still don't know if you can meet up with Steve."

"We can call the hotel where he's going to be next— but not from here," Abby added quickly. "The police have the phone tapped, which is why I asked both of you to come over."

"Tell them we persuaded you to spend the night with us," he suggested. "They'll buy that."

Abby gave him a grateful nod and went to make a brief call to Angel, who seemed relieved that she wasn't going to be alone. Then she went upstairs and threw some clothes into a suitcase, conscious that she might be packing for a trip halfway around the world.

"IT'S NOT TOO LATE to back out," Noel Zacharias's words rang in Abby's ears as the trio stepped off the escalator at Baltimore-Washington International Airport.

Abby gave her friend a wry grin as she realized what strange tricks fate could play. "Didn't we have a similar scene a couple of months ago? Only you were the one who was going off on the harebrained adventure. The difference is, *you* didn't know you'd be hooking up with Jason."

They all laughed self-consciously. Then Noel reached for her husband's hand.

"Everything worked out for the two of you," Abby whispered. "So it has to for me."

She clung to that thought during the exhausting eighteen-hour flight that took her to New Delhi, India.

Luckily, she'd been to this country before on a visit with Steve, so she'd already had a valid passport and most of the inoculations she needed. But even before she'd cleared customs, she was struck once again with how foreign the environment seemed. The feeling of total immersion in another world grew on the taxi ride from the airport into the city. The very air was different, hot and humid and pungent with the smell of exotic spices and something earthy. When she'd asked Steve what she was smelling, he'd laughed and told her it was the burning dung the populations used for fuel. At first she'd been repulsed, yet it really wasn't unpleasant.

The foreign odors wafted in through the open windows of the ancient Chevy, along with a cacophony of noises. The grinding gears of buses and trucks. The shouts of vendors along the street. The babble of voices in a dozen languages—most of which she didn't understand. Yet now and then a few words of musically accented English drifted toward her.

It had all seemed so much safer with Steve at her side to smooth the way. Today she felt lost as she jounced along on a seat from which half the stuffing must be missing. A hole that was covered with a coarse blanket scratched against her thighs.

Leaning back, Abby closed her eyes. She was exhausted by the long trip and the ten hour time difference. Alone and fighting a sense of confusion, she tried to will her tense muscles to relax as the taxi wove its way through the crowded streets. But her pulse continued to thrum.

What if she'd missed Steve? What if he'd already left for Oliver Gibbs's other hideout? The one in the jungle.

And what if she had to face something even worse? What if her husband didn't want her here? She'd acted as if he were deserting her; or as if she'd thought he was escaping from reality. Would he understand why she hadn't been able to cope with the enormity of his conclusions?

To stop the questions chasing each other through her head, she turned back to practical matters. Jason had called ahead and left a message to be given to Mr. Claiborne when he arrived at the hotel. She hoped his words had filtered through the crackling telephone connection and the imprecise English of the hotel clerk on the other end of the line.

Abby still had many miles to travel before even that question was answered. It was a long ride from the airport to the suburb where Steve was staying. Apparently he'd chosen a location along the route to Oliver's.

As the sun set, the air cooled a little. Looking out the window, Abby could see they had come fairly far from the center of the city. The buildings were no longer packed one against the other but interspersed among cultivated fields with crops she couldn't name.

She was wondering how much farther it would be when the vehicle finally pulled in between tall white pillars, one of which bore a brass plaque. It was lighted and Abby could make out the words Akbar Hotel. The narrow driveway wound through beds of swaying red and yellow flowers. The building was long and low, with turrets and balconies and a portico that bordered a rectangular, reflecting pool.

As soon as the taxi stopped, a uniformed doorman rushed forward to grab the door handle.

"Welcome to the Akbar, Missy."

Abby fumbled in her purse for unfamiliar bills and coins to pay the fare. Jason had gotten the money for her right after he'd arranged her flight to Frankfurt and then east. He'd also made sure her medical records were in order. Abby had realized gratefully that no one else besides her husband would have been able to smooth her way so easily.

Squaring her shoulders, she got out of the cab. At least Steve had booked himself first-class accommodations. The exterior was beautifully kept. The lobby was cool and spacious—an oasis of marble floors, Oriental rugs and heavy wicker furniture.

Yet even first-class hotels had their problems. Abby found herself at the front desk behind a businessman from Djakarta who became furious when told he didn't have a reservation. Swaying with exhaustion but afraid to get out of line, she waited twenty minutes while the clerk and a manager straightened out the mess.

Then it was Abby's turn. She gave her name and gripped the counter with rigid fingers while the woman checked the files.

"Your room is ready, Mrs. Claiborne."

Abby relaxed her death grip on the polished marble. "Has my husband arrived yet?"

"We were expecting him this afternoon, but he hasn't checked in yet."

A porter led her down a wide, dimly lit corridor toward the back of the hotel. Her room overlooked a walled garden where bougainvillea festooned a high stucco wall. At the base were Queen of the Nile lilies. After giving the room and the view the briefest of glances, she drew the drapes and pulled off her skirt and blouse.

In the bathroom she turned on the shower before she could tell herself that she was too tired for anything but bed. Besides, her breasts ached, and she needed to express some milk. It would have been a lot easier to simply let the supply dry up, but that would have been breaking one of her last remaining links with Shannon. When they found her daughter, she was going to nurse her again.

Twenty minutes later she was feeling clean and a lot more comfortable. After throwing on a cotton gown from her suitcase, she climbed between the sheets of the double bed and burrowed down against the air-conditioned chill of the room. Almost as soon as her head hit the pillow, she was asleep.

FOUR HUNDRED MILES to the west, Amarjit Singh was too restless to sleep. Too many responsibilities weighed on his shoulders. A powerfully built man with dark curly hair and a beard to match, brown eyes, and sun-bronzed skin, he was a leader who commanded respect as much for his intellect as for his size.

His followers called him the Lion. The government had labeled him a terrorist. In reality, Singh was a practical man who could order a kidnapping or assassination with the same ruthless ease as the bombing of a public office building during business hours.

Singh balled up the communiqué he'd received a few minutes ago and tossed it disgustedly across his Russian-army-issue tent. There was still no sign of the American, Steve Claiborne. He wasn't in Baltimore or India. At least as far as anyone knew. He had simply vanished, and that was very unfortunate. He was counting on Claiborne to track down Oliver Gibbs and recover the lost cargo before it was too late.

The fall elections were only weeks away, and the shipment Gibbs had stolen was his best chance of getting the concessions the Indian Liberation Army sought from a government that was deaf, dumb, and blind to the plight of the Sikhs.

Singh stared out the door of the tent at the moonlit sky. Ten years ago he'd had nothing more on his mind than his engineering studies at Punjab University, but all that changed the day a thousand protestors—including his own father—were murdered at the Golden Temple. The tragedy had hardened his heart, and over the past few years he'd come to believe that any means justified the ends he sought.

He brought his attention back to the present. He might have lost Claiborne for the moment, but the man would turn up soon—if he ever wanted to see his daughter again.

"The bird is landing, *jathedār*," a young recruit informed him.

The Lion rose from the intricately patterned rug that lined his tent. The accommodations—a sleeping mat, washbowl, kerosene lamp, and rattan chest for his few clothes—were Spartan by western standards. But his people were used to a simple way of life, even if this desert stronghold was a recent variation.

On the other hand, the nomadic encampments made a strange contrast to the modern equipment necessary to wage a successful guerilla offensive. In the compound, other tents housed arms, medical supplies and communications equipment, including radios, Teletype machines, and rugged field computers—most of which had been acquired from U.S. companies through third parties, or had been left by the Soviets when they'd vacated Pakistan.

Amarjit stepped into the night air, which had fallen thirty degrees from the 110-degree heat of day.

The whirling noise grew louder as a Soviet-made helicopter approached from the east. In the moonlight, he watched the bird land on the flat sands bordering the encampment. When the blades stopped moving, a woman carrying a small bundle got out. Sunita, the wife of his youth. She was from the city, a woman whose parents had educated their daughter almost as well as their sons. His hopes had been high when he'd married her. Now her use to him was limited. Yet perhaps only she could have stolen the hostage for him.

"Bring them to my tent at once," he told his first lieutenant.

Ten minutes later, a woman's shadow blocked the light. "You sent for me, master?"

"Yes. Enter."

Obediently Sunita moved into the tent. She was holding the babe securely in her arms.

"The child tolerated the journey?"

"As well as could be expected for such a tiny infant." The little girl started to cry, and Sunita rocked her gently.

Amarjit's dark eyes narrowed as he observed the protective way Sunita hugged the other woman's baby. He could have cast this woman aside when she'd failed to provide him with an heir, but he'd kept her around even after he'd taken another wife, and twisted her shortcomings to his advantage.

"You have done well."

"Thank you, my husband."

"You can turn the babe over to Veena."

"No, please. I know how to care for her."

"You question my orders?"

Sunita's eyes focused on a spot near his feet. "No, Lion of our people. I would never do that. You know I have done everything you asked of me," she said in a small voice. "In the American hospital, I received special training. I can keep her well for you."

He studied her bent head. "Yes, your part was most important in our plans. By the grace of Akāl, we will be victorious in winning freedom for our Land of the Pure, Khālistān."

"By Akāl's grace," she repeated.

"Show me the child."

Sunita stepped forward and unfolded the light cotton blanket, revealing the tiny little girl.

Amarjit stared at her, not so much seeing the infant as the bargaining power she represented. Purposefully, he unsheathed his sword and tested the razor-sharp edge. Then he brought down the weapon mere inches from the small, vulnerable head. He could see Sunita's arms tremble as he demonstrated his power over the baby—and over her. But she didn't back away.

He could kill this girl child as easily as he could swat an insect. But she was valuable to her parents. With one swift stoke, he cut off a lock of the fine baby hair, then replaced the sword. "You may keep the hostage for now. But do not become too attached to her. Remember, she is only a means to an end."

"Thank you, Lion of our people."

Her tone was submissive, but he detected a defiant note that she was doing her best to hide. He'd sent Sunita on other missions to the west. Each time she returned, he saw the contact had undermined her upbringing. She'd bear watching.

"Go rest now. You have had a long journey."

After bowing to his command, she hurried from the tent.

He closed his large fist around the baby's hair. He had the child. He would use her to bend the parents to his will. He would send them this token with his next communication.

ONE MOMENT Abby was asleep, tucked under the covers with her knees drawn up like a little animal snug in its den. Then a sound woke her. In the darkness, she didn't know where she was and felt panic expand in her chest. Her hand darted out, and she reached for the light switch beside the bed. But her fingers brushed only plaster. Rough plaster.

Her heart began to thump.

Don't lose your cool. If you figure out where you are, everything will be okay.

Abby dredged up a hazy vision of an unfamiliar hotel room. In India. The Akbar. For confirmation, she rolled toward the finger of silvery light where the window curtains didn't quite meet.

She drew in a steadying breath and let it out slowly. She was perfectly all right. She'd locked the door as soon as the porter had left. But she'd been so tired she couldn't remember slipping the security chain into place.

Her nerves jangled again. In the darkness, the room felt wrong.

As if another presence waited in the shadows.

Her breath stilled, and her ears probed the darkness. She was half convinced she could hear the sound of breathing—and half convinced that she was imagining it.

Yet she couldn't just lie there waiting for someone to pounce. Moving stealthily, Abby began to slide toward the far side of the bed. Before she'd crossed more than a few inches, a large, hard hand clamped itself over her mouth.

She tried to scream, tried to wrench away, but the owner of the hand was far stronger than she. In desperation, she began to lash her head from side to side. He simply pulled her against his hard chest, smothering her in a sweaty shirtfront. She worked her mouth against the damp fabric. When her teeth dug into his flesh, he grunted and shook her roughly.

"All right, let's find out what the hell's going on." His weight shifted as he dragged her back across the bed.

When she heard his voice, she tried desperately to speak, but that was still impossible. Now her goal was to keep him from hurting her as he yanked her fully out from under the covers. However, her knees gave way as they hit the floor.

"Stand up, damn it."

The sheet tangled around her legs and trailed along behind her as he half carried, half pulled her across the wide floorboards toward the door. What was he going to do, throw her out into the hall?

With one hand, he turned her face toward his. With the other, he threw the switch, flooding the room with light.

She blinked as she stared up into Steve's startled blue eyes. His astonished exclamation mingled with her sob of relief as he unclamped his hand from her mouth.

"Abby!"

On another sob, she collapsed against him, her arms winding around his shoulders, her face pressing against his neck. He held her tightly, his hands stroking unsteadily across her back.

"Abby?" he repeated. "What . . . what are you doing here?"

When she lifted her face to his again, he wiped a hand across his eyes, staring at her as if he didn't believe she was real. His gaze went from her bloodless features to the nightgown twisted around her body and gaping away from her right shoulder. With shaky fingers, he smoothed it back into place, smothering a self-deprecating curse under his breath. "God, I'm sorry. D-did I hurt you?"

"No." She searched his eyes. They were shadowed with fatigue. "Who did you think I was?"

He shrugged. "God knows. I picked this place because I've never been here before—it's not the kind of hotel I'd normally choose. I guess I thought someone had figured out where I was." He laughed hollowly. "An assassin. Someone sent to get information from me. Your mind can spin some great fantasies when you've been running on no sleep as long as I have."

"Nobody told you I was coming? Or that I'd arrived?"

"As far as I knew, I was the only one checked in to this room." He looked over Abby's shoulder at the covers strewn across the floor. "When I saw a shape in my bed, I just reacted."

She nodded.

"There isn't even a night clerk at the desk," he continued. "Probably because they don't expect guests to show up at 4:00 a.m. I had to get the porter to tell me which room I was in."

"But they were supposed to give you a message from Jason."

She saw him go very still. Then his hands dug painfully into her shoulders. "A message? Did you come here to break bad news—" He swallowed hard. "Did they find Shannon's body—?"

"No. Not that! Nothing like that," Abby reassured him quickly. She *had* come with bad news, but not that bad.

He stared down into her eyes. "Then what? What brought you all this way when you told me I was going on a wild-goose chase?"

She clutched at his arms. "Oh, Steve. I should have listened to you. You were right about Mrs. Hamadi." The anguished words tumbled from her lips. "I was crazy enough to feel sorry for her, but she didn't take Shannon because she wanted a baby. Or if she did, that's only part of it. She...she was working for someone else."

Abby leaned heavily against Steve, and he swung her up into his embrace, carrying her across the room to one of the armchairs by the window. Sitting down, he cradled her in his lap. She wanted to huddle there with her eyes closed, as if being in his arms again would make this nightmare go away. But the sharp edge in his voice brought her back to reality.

"Who is she working for?"

"Terrorists," Abby wheezed. "A group called the Indian Liberation Army. Jason says they want to overthrow the Indian government."

A curse exploded from Steve's lips. "How do you know it's them? Is that what the police found out?"

"No. They sent me a note warning me not to work with the police, or contact the CIA."

"A note?"

"And a picture of Shannon. They're in my luggage."

Crossing the room on shaky legs, she found the envelope and brought it back to Steve. First he studied the picture.

"She...she looks okay," Abby whispered, dropping to her knees beside him. "I think they're taking good care of her." She didn't know that for sure, but it was what she wanted to believe.

Quickly he read the message. When he finished, he swore again.

Abby gripped his knee. "You were right about the connection to Oliver. And I was wrong. Oh, Steve, I should have listened to you."

"I'm not exactly batting a thousand."

She raised her gaze to his face, taking in the lines of strain around his eyes and mouth. "Jason showed me your flight plan. You went to Borneo."

"Yeah. Oliver wasn't there." He shook his head wearily. "I've been flying a plane for six hours—after a couple of days tramping through the jungle on a wild-goose chase."

"What happened?"

"The mayor of the village where Oliver was living gave me what sounded like a cock-and-bull story, but I had to follow it up, just in case." He sighed. "Ollie is an expert at covering his tracks. He wasted a hell of a lot of my time and energy. When I get my hands on him, I'm going to wring his neck."

Abby could see that his loyalty to his friend had been worn a bit thin by recent events. "You said Oliver had two hideouts. If he wasn't in Borneo, then he's near here," she pressed.

"He sure as hell better be."

Abby dragged in a shuddering breath. "The ILA won't hurt Shannon while they think they can get what they want out of you! That gives us time to rescue her." There was no use even asking Steve whether he thought the rebel leader could be trusted to give their daughter back once he'd secured his merchandise. She knew they couldn't count on that. "And Oliver will tell you what's going on," she finished.

She tried to cling to that conviction, even as she thought about the smiling, wisecracking man they'd had dinner with on their last trip to India. He'd been charming and fun, but she'd been glad she didn't have to rely on him for anything—not after some of the hair-raising stories he'd told. She felt her chest tighten painfully. Oliver Gibbs might hold her child's life in his hands. How much would he care about Shannon?

"He's got to help us," Abby muttered.

"Yeah." There was a steely edge in Steve's voice. He wouldn't just ask for Oliver's assistance. He'd *make* him cooperate.

"We'll talk to him tomorrow."

"Abby, I don't know what I'll find out when I get to his place. Hell, for all I know, he's got a bunch of new business associates who are calling the shots. It would be safer if you stayed here. It would be even safer for you if you went home."

She wanted to protest, but the look on Steve's face stopped her. He had been traveling constantly for almost three days. As of now, he was no closer to finding Oliver than when he'd left Baltimore. The last thing he needed tonight was an argument from her. What he needed was her warmth and comfort, even if he was too strung out and too exhausted to ask for them.

He was watching her tensely. When she didn't protest, a tiny measure of the anguish seeped out of his eyes.

"I'm frightened, the way I was when I was a little girl and woke up after a nightmare. I—I need to be held," she whispered.

"Abby." He opened his arms, and she climbed back into his lap and laid her head against his shoulder. For her it was a simple, basic gesture, natural and right.

She felt a shudder go through Steve's body as his hands tightened on her shoulders. She'd been loved and protected as a little girl, assured that she was important and valuable to her parents. Steve had been born to wealth, but he'd never had the simple luxury of knowing his parents cared.

She knew what that kind of deprivation could do to a child. She knew exactly what it had done to this man. When they'd first met, asking for love and comfort had been alien concepts to him.

He pressed his face against the top of her head, sighing out a long, unsteady breath. She burrowed closer to his warmth and felt his hands stroking over her arms and shoulders. They sat for long moments— a husband and wife silently sharing the worst crisis of their lives. It was almost too much to bear. The only way to do it was together. And tomorrow she'd make him understand that. Tonight she was too exhausted to speak, too exhausted to do more than cling to him.

She could hear the steady beat of his heart under her ear, strong and vital and comforting. Her eyes fluttered closed. For the first time in days she felt a little of the terrible pressure in her chest ease. And then she was asleep.

Chapter Six

Only a narrow shaft of light knifed through the crack in the curtains. Yet Steve knew exactly where he was when he woke, and who was beside him in the wide, unfamiliar hotel bed.

Abby was nestled under the covers with him, her head almost touching his arm, her breast inches from his hand. In that desperate moment of awakening when his guard was down, he felt his whole body throb with wanting her.

He closed his eyes, but that didn't lessen the need. Every one of his senses was tuned to her. His head was filled with her sweet, familiar scent. His ears were picking up little else but the gentle sound of her breathing. And the warmth of her body made him want to surge forward and gather her close.

His eyes blinked open again. As his vision became accustomed to the dim light, his gaze roamed over her, taking in the sweep of dark lashes hiding her eyes, the rich brown hair tangled around her shoulders, the pale, almost translucent color of her skin. Sleep had eased the tense set of her lips that had made his throat constrict so painfully the night before, but it hadn't erased the shadows under her eyes.

She'd fallen asleep in his arms last night. And she hadn't even stirred when he'd laid her on the bed and pulled the covers up around her. How much rest had she gotten in the past few days? Probably not a lot.

As he gazed at his wife, his throat closed again. He wanted her. Needed her. But how could he be thinking about making love to her now? Now, when he knew she was exhausted and when the daughter he'd barely met was missing, kidnapped by a group of thugs who might do God knows what.

But maybe that was precisely why he needed Abby so much. Once it would have been impossible for him to admit that he cared about anyone's emotional support. Yet the whole time he'd been gone, he'd imagined seeing her, holding her, drawing comfort from her—easing his pain in her arms.

But as he lay there watching her sleep, thinking about the past three days, he couldn't imagine why she would want to give him anything. This whole mess they were in was his fault for teaming up with such an irresponsible hothead as Ollie Gibbs.

His jaw clenched to the point of pain. God, couldn't he do anything right?

A desperate fantasy flashed into his mind. He could see himself easing out of the bed, finding his clothes and disappearing before Abby woke up. Then he'd drag ol' Ollie back here and make him explain to Abby exactly what had happened. Except that if he went looking for him alone, he might kill him.

The Indian Liberation Army. Didn't Gibbs know how dangerous, how unpredictable, they were? And what had he done—double-cross them? What the hell was he thinking about? Steve's teeth grated against each other.

Abby stirred beside him, and his eyes were instantly on her again. Her features contorted, and she moaned softly in her sleep.

"Sweetheart?"

Her head moved from side to side on the pillow. Then a look of fear etched itself into her face.

"Don't!" he murmured as he reached out to cup her shoulders. The moment his hands touched her flesh, her lids fluttered, and those large green eyes sought his.

Time seemed to hang suspended, as if the world had suddenly stopped spinning on its axis.

"Abby?"

She didn't speak, but a pulse began to pound in her throat. His gaze shifted from her face to that spot of pulsing flesh and back again, and he felt his own body throbbing in the same rhythm. He heard a soft moan like the one she'd made in her sleep, and his whole body tensed. Then she closed the space between them, sliding her arms around his neck and pulling him against the length of her body.

"I need you, Steve. I need you. Don't leave me like that again."

"Oh, Lord, sweetheart. I'm sorry. I'm so sorry. I didn't know what else to do."

His embrace enveloped her even as she gathered him close. He told himself he just wanted to give her comfort, like last night.

Then she lifted her mouth to find his, and every other thought was driven from his head.

"I need you," she tried to say again. He couldn't hear the words, but he felt them.

His mouth moved feverishly over hers. Hers did the same as they shared a deep, desperate kiss. It was the kiss of a man and woman reaching out to each other on the most basic of levels. A kiss that asked and gave reassurances where words might never be enough. But more than that, it was a kiss of lovers too long parted, too long denied, too long frustrated.

Teeth, tongues, lips. They sought each other in every way that two mouths could make contact. Could give and take pleasure. He drew in her warm breath and gave it back as he sighed her name.

Suddenly the thin cotton gown she wore was an intolerable barrier. He pulled it up and over her head, tossing it onto the floor, even as he began to shed his own briefs. Then he pulled her hot, yielding flesh against his, and they began to rock as if caught in a great rolling surge on an endless sea.

Every inch of his body registered erotic sensations. The twin pressure of her breasts against his chest. The sliding caress of her smooth leg hooked around his rougher one. The way his erection nestled in the cleft between her legs as their bodies cleaved together.

She gasped at the intimate contact, and they both went very still.

"I'd forgotten," she murmured. "How could I have forgotten?"

He knew exactly what she was talking about. It was a long time since the bulky contour of her body had let them lie this way, face-to-face, her shape molded so sensually to his. Not that making love while she was pregnant hadn't been good. But the new sleekness of her figure was startlingly provoking.

Slowly, his fingertips skimmed along her velvety skin, tracing up her hip, dipping in at the hollow of her waist, and coming to rest on her right breast. He gently rolled her onto her back and trailed his knuckles across her breasts, following the sensuous path with his eyes. Her breasts were rounder, fuller than before, the nipples larger and darker. He watched admiringly as they responded to his touch, felt his body tighten as he heard her little indrawn breath.

Coming down beside her, he curled the tip of his tongue around one beautifully hardened nipple. "Can I?"

She flushed as her eyes met his. Then she opened her arms to him.

When he took her in his mouth and began to suck, he felt her arch. Her hands came up to clasp his head, and she made a long, low sound he felt in every cell of his body.

"Sweet," he murmured as he moved his mouth from one nipple to the other. "Sweet." At the same time, his hand stroked her most intimate flesh. She was warm and wet and very ready for him.

"Steve. I want...I need you...now."

"Is it all right? Will I hurt you?"

"I don't know."

When he shifted on top of her, he felt her hand grasp his distended length to guide him. But as he began to press into her, she winced.

He went very still above her, staring down into the deep green of her eyes.

"Don't stop. Please don't stop."

"Sweetheart, wait. We can—"

"No. I need you." Her hips arched and her fingers dug into his hips, urging him forward. She gasped as he came inside her, the sound tearing at his soul.

He was afraid to move, afraid of hurting her any more. "Abby?"

She stirred beneath him. Then she was kissing his face, reaching for his lips with hers, even as she began to rock her hips against him.

"So long. It's been so long."

Long, lonely weeks when they'd needed each other and had been denied this comfort, this fulfillment, this vitally important part of their marriage.

Another gasp tore from her throat, but this time was very different. Now he heard pleasure in her voice, not pain. She held nothing back, moving, moaning, mingling her essence with his. And as she drove toward her climax she fueled his.

He cried out her name in a tone he hardly recognized, gathering her tightly against him as his body lost itself in hers.

IN THE AFTERMATH, Abby wanted to drift for a little while longer in a cloud of peace and contentment. Steve belonged to her. No one could steal him away from her the way they'd—

Not yet. Don't make me face reality yet.

Above her, he stirred, shifting his weight off her body. "I didn't want to hurt you," he whispered, his mouth buried in the thick curtain of her hair.

She turned her face, caressing his cheek with her lips. "I didn't want you to stop. I wasn't going to let you stop." She drew in a shallow breath. "And it only hurt right at the beginning. After that, it was wonderful."

He didn't move, and she stroked her fingers across his broad shoulders. "Don't feel guilty. About anything."

She heard him swallow. "You mean about liking that so much when we don't know where Shannon is."

"Steve, I came here for two reasons. Because I need to help you get our daughter back. And because I need to be with you every way I can be with you."

He lifted his face and looked down at her. "Being here is putting you in danger. All of this is happening because I was stupid enough to say yes when Gibbs asked if I wanted to be his partner.''

''Steve, that was a long time ago, before you ever met me. Teaming up with Oliver was the right thing for you to do at the time, wasn't it?''

He nodded tightly.

''I know you're angry with him now. But don't let that poison your good memories, or make you question your judgment. You gave up your business out here to marry me. And you're not responsible for what Oliver did after you left.''

''I can't change the way I feel.''

A small smile flickered around her lips. ''Well, not without a dozen or so counseling sessions. And I didn't come out here for that. I came because I can't just sit at home and wait for you to make things come out right. I have to help. Because I love you. And Shannon.''

''I love you, too.''

She held him fiercely against her breasts.

''Do you know what it would do to me if something happened to you because you're with me now?'' he whispered.

''You said we can't trust the ILA. I could be sitting at home in Baltimore, and they could decide they want another hostage. They didn't have any trouble finding me a couple of days ago. They broke into the house to leave the ransom note. It was in the middle of our bed. I think I'm as safe with you as anywhere else.''

He swore low and angrily, and rolled onto his back, staring up at the ceiling. ''You mean, either way I've put my wife and child at risk.''

''No! Stop feeling guilty. Weren't you paying any attention to what I was saying? You didn't have any control over what Oliver chose to do after you pulled out of the business and came back home." She rested her cheek against his chest, listening to the drumming beat of his heart. Then she lifted her head so that she could look down into his troubled eyes. "It's been a terrible six weeks—for both of us. And I haven't made it any better."

"Abby—"

"You...you were apprehensive about being a father. Then after Shannon was born, I was so worried that I didn't know how to stop focusing on her and help you deal with your feelings. And when she was kidnapped, I couldn't let myself accept your assessment of what had happened."

"Take your own advice, and stop feeling guilty."

She stroked her knuckles against his jaw. "I can't, if you can't be open with me."

"I was pretty open with you a few minutes ago."

"That's different."

He combed his fingers through her hair, but the silence between them lengthened. "Abby, it's a lot for me to cope with," he finally whispered.

"I know. God, I know."

"We'll find her, and bring her back. That's the most important thing right now. That's the level I have to work on."

Abby buried her face against his shoulder and held fast to him for a few minutes longer. When his arms tightened around her, she squeezed her eyes shut. She wanted her daughter back—more than anything in the world. But what if the unthinkable happened? What if they couldn't find Shannon? Would Steve turn away from her in guilt and despair? If she lost her daughter, would she lose her husband, too?

STEVE DROVE the Range Rover he'd rented toward a line of low hills. The transportation was a lot more comfortable than the taxi she'd been in the evening before, and Abby leaned back in the bucket seat and stretched out her legs.

At first the countryside was covered with low bushes and trees interspersed with cultivated fields. But as they drove farther from the city, the vegetation became more lush and the signs of habitation more sparse. Before she'd come to India the first time, Abby had pictured every square inch of the country as heavily populated. But that wasn't true.

She pulled her gaze away from the unfamiliar trees gliding past the window and focused on the rigid set of Steve's jaw. He caught her watching him and reached to cover her hand.

"How are you feeling?" he asked.

"Okay. How are you? Are you still upset that I came?"

"No. I was thinking about Ollie. It's probably lucky that you're with me. You can keep me from choking the life out of him."

Abby turned her palm up and knit her fingers with Steve's. She knew her husband pretty well by now. With his child in danger, he needed to be angry at someone, and Oliver Gibbs was the most convenient candidate. For her, it was Mrs. Hamadi. At first she'd felt sorry for the woman. Now she wanted to shake her by the shoulders until she confessed what she'd done with Shannon.

"How much farther?" she asked.

"Three or four hours, if the roads hold up."

Abby wanted to drive straight through, but even in the Range Rover, it was hard to sit still for so long.

"I got the hotel to pack us some lunch," Steve said as the sun approached its zenith. "Let's find a place to eat."

He stopped by an outcropping of rocks where a little stream cascaded under a low, rickety bridge.

Getting out, she stretched her legs. Steve had brought extra gasoline along, because there were no filling stations in this part of the country. There were no rest rooms, either, so he waited while she reconnoitered the woods.

As she followed the narrow trail he'd indicated, she looked around at the shiny green vegetation and the bright flowers standing out like dots of yellow and orange neon among the leaves. In the underbrush, insects buzzed. Somewhere in the trees above, birds objected to her intrusion.

As she looked up to find them, she caught sight of a family of monkeys chattering as they moved away.

Shannon would have enjoyed that. When they had their daughter back, they'd come here again, she told herself, striving to hold on to the light mood. They'd sit here quietly and the birds and animals would come back.

When Abby emerged once more, Steve had spread a madras cloth and laid out the food. The hotel had given them flat bread called *nan,* spicy vegetable salad, chutney, and tandoori chicken.

Steve watched Abby nibble at a piece of bread. "You've got to eat more than that."

"I know."

She noticed he'd taken chicken but wasn't mustering much more enthusiasm for the food than she. "So how do you think Oliver got mixed up with the ILA?" she asked.

Steve sighed. "They probably offered him a hefty payment for flying low and avoiding the border patrols."

"Bringing in what?"

"Weapons. Amarjit Singh wants to overthrow the central government—or at least destabilize it so that the local regions have more autonomy. Over the past five or six years, his group has claimed the credit for a number of assassinations. Maybe they're planning something bigger."

"According to their ransom note, Oliver still has whatever he was supposed to transport. Why?"

"Well, unless he's changed, he's not a thief. The only thing I can figure is that *they* double-crossed him. Maybe they tried to take delivery without paying for the job. Or maybe there was a mix-up about the price. I know Oliver. If he thought he was being cheated, he'd keep the merchandise."

"Didn't he realize he was taking a big risk?"

"I guess he thought he could get away with it—that he could stay out of their clutches. Meanwhile, he'd be able to locate another buyer."

Abby froze. "Another buyer? But then how can we get the stuff back?"

Steve looked as if he wished he hadn't spoken so quickly, but his voice was reassuring. "I was just speculating. Besides, we're not talking about selling electric can openers. It takes the right contacts to unload sophisticated weapons."

"Anyway, he didn't think you were going to get involved."

"Maybe he took the ILA job because they offered him enough to clear his note with me," Steve grated.

Abby moved over several inches so that her shoulder was touching his. She knew about Steve's relation-

ship with Oliver. Steve had come to India looking for
a life as different as possible from the corporate poli-
tics and infighting of his family's business in Baltimore. Oliver had recognized him as a kindred spirit—
a man willing to take risks if they made him feel alive.

They'd worked well together. They'd taken chances,
made money and led comfortable lives as exiles in an
exotic culture. Steve might talk as if he were furious
with Oliver Gibbs. But, even if he couldn't admit it to
himself, he was probably wondering how he could help
his old friend out of a mess and still save his daughter.

Abby hooked her arm around his waist. She hoped
there was some way to do both. If not, she knew
Shannon came first. With both of them.

It was almost three by the time they reached the un-
pretentious turnoff to the property Oliver had pur-
chased outside of a little agricultural village. It wasn't
where he lived all year 'round. In fact, he'd always kept
the location private for when he needed a place to lie
low. Several hundred feet from the road, an airstrip
rose above what must have once been a rice field. Steve
pulled up beside the corrugated metal hangar. Inside
was a twin-engine plane.

"He's here!" Abby crowed.

"One of his planes is here," Steve corrected as he
went to look inside the cockpit. But he appeared satisfied when he climbed back behind the wheel. And
Abby felt some of the terrible tension that had been in
her chest all day ease a little.

They continued up a hill, and she caught a glimpse
of a house through the trees.

Steve sped up, then slammed on the brakes as he
came around a curve. The back end of an old Land
Rover was half blocking the rutted road. The front

bumper was buried in the underbrush. Getting out, he peered into the vehicle.

"It's Oliver's. And I can see some boxes inside."

The windows of the vehicle were rolled up tight, but the door wasn't locked. Steve opened it and stepped back quickly.

"What?"

He coughed and slammed the door. But a heavy, fetid odor was already drifting toward Abby, and several flies plastered themselves against the window.

Steve pulled a dry branch from a nearby mimosa. Abby's stomach knotted as she watched him avert his face and open the door again. The flies rushed in, settling on the nearest box. Extending his arm and using the stick, Steve lifted the flap and peered inside.

"Rotten fruit. And vegetables," he reported as he slammed the door again.

Abby stared at the box, knowing she'd expected him to find something much worse. "Why would he leave a bunch of food to rot?"

"Because he left in a hurry and didn't come back. The question is, why?" He looked at Abby as he slipped behind the wheel of their Rover. "Maybe you'd better wait here."

"From the smell of that stuff, it's been in there for weeks, so I think we can assume no one's holding him hostage in his bedroom. Maybe he wanted it to look as if he cleared out in a rush." Abby swallowed. "Or maybe that's exactly what he did. Maybe we're too late."

Steve eased their vehicle around Oliver's Land Rover. Then he pressed his foot down on the accelerator. The wheels spun on the gravel as they lurched forward.

Abby held her breath, hoping they wouldn't run into any more obstacles along the narrow road. Luckily, the rest of the way up the hill was clear.

As they rounded the last curve, they came face-to-face with the dwelling. It was larger than it had appeared from the main road and was surrounded by gardens and verandas situated to take the best advantage of the view. The effect would have been charming, except that the place had a forlorn, neglected look. The flower beds were choked with weeds, and debris littered the surface of the verandas.

Steve cut the motor, reached into the back seat and grabbed a bag that looked as though it was designed to carry gym shoes. Instead of a pair of sneakers, however, he pulled out a snub-nosed pistol.

Abby stared at the weapon. "Where...where did you get that?"

"A place I know in New Delhi."

"You don't think Oliver—"

"I don't know what to think. He may not be here at all. There's a place up in the jungle where he could be hiding out, but I'm going to check the house first." Cutting off further conversation, he opened the door and started for the front porch, gun in hand.

Abby followed closely behind him, unable to shake the sense that something was terribly wrong.

They climbed the steps, their footsteps ringing hollowly on the wooden boards. Steve knocked on the front door. After waiting half a minute for an answer, he turned the knob and pushed.

The door swung inward on unused hinges and a wave of heat wafted toward them. It was accompanied by an odor not unlike the rotten fruit and vegetables. Abby shrank back. This time she was pretty sure they weren't smelling produce left too long in a hot vehicle.

She glanced at Steve.

"Stay here."

"No."

He stepped across the threshold and she followed. "Ollie?"

The silent house gave no reply.

"I wonder what happened to the servants," Steve mused.

He didn't suggest they split up and search. Instead they began to move through the house together, starting with the sitting room. Oliver favored comfortable wicker furniture with subdued upholstery, Oriental rugs, and brass ornaments. Under different circumstances, Abby would have commented favorably on his taste.

Her tension grew as they walked from room to empty room and then down a short hall. Unlike the unkempt exterior, the inside of the house was spotless, as if someone had tidied up before going on vacation.

"This is his bedroom," Steve said in a low voice, stopping before a closed door.

It was the only one that wasn't opened, and Abby's stomach clenched.

Steve must have felt the same sense of foreboding, because his hand hesitated on the knob. Then he stepped inside. When he uttered a low exclamation, she tried to peer around his shoulder.

"What?"

He didn't answer but moved aside, his eyes fixed on the wide bed about ten feet from where they stood.

Abby followed his gaze and felt herself go sick and cold all over. In the center of the mattress, huddled like a frightened child under the cotton coverlet, was a wizened body. A corpse.

Chapter Seven

"Oh, Lord, no." Abby grabbed at Steve's arm, but he was already moving toward the bed. "Is it Oliver?"

Several seconds passed before he answered her question. "Who else could it be?"

Almost against her will, Abby stepped forward and saw what hadn't been apparent from the doorway. A gun was cradled against the man's chest and a rust-colored stain discolored the front of his dirty khaki shirt. She must have swayed on her feet, because Steve's arm came up to support her weight.

"Steady."

She leaned heavily against him, breathing shallowly. She wanted to get out of the room. Out of the house. Away from the lifeless thing on the bed. Instead she tried to take in more details.

She had met Oliver Gibbs a couple of times and remembered him as a tall, lively individual, with a boyish grin and curly black hair just going gray at the temples. Now it was hard to comprehend that she was looking at the same man. The dry heat inside the house must have mummified his corpse, shrinking his body. His skin had turned dark and leathery and was molded against his skull so that he looked as if he'd been closer to ninety than forty. The aging effect was exaggerated by his hair—or rather, the lack of it. Only a few strands still clung to the top of his head. The rest was gone, some of it lying like a dark halo on the pillow.

"He looks like he's been dead for centuries. Like a body in an ancient tomb," Abby whispered.

Steve nodded. Then, as if he had suddenly realized he was holding a pistol, he tucked the weapon into the waistband of his jeans. "Come on, let's get out of here."

The words released a tide of sickness in Abby's throat. Gagging, she turned and practically ran back the way they had come. Outside, she gulped in a deep draft of air.

Steve opened the door of the Range Rover, and she dropped onto the seat. As she leaned back against the headrest, she felt cold sweat collecting on her body.

Steve squatted beside her right knee, and she reached for his shoulder, gripping it tightly.

"What do we do now?" she whispered.

"You're going to sit here and try to feel better. I'm going back inside."

"No!"

"I've got to see if he's left a note—or anything that would explain what's happened."

Abby swallowed. She should help search, but now that she was outside in the sunshine and open air, she knew she couldn't force herself back inside.

"Are you going to be okay?" Steve asked.

"Yes."

He pulled the gun from his waistband. "You keep this."

"Why?"

"Just in case. I won't need it in there."

When Steve had insisted she learn to use a gun, she'd thought he was being paranoid. Now...

Abby sat with the weapon cradled in her lap as she watched him climb the stairs. When he disappeared inside, she pressed her fist against her mouth to keep from crying out.

In a kind of numb haze, she kept picturing the almost inhuman thing they'd found on the bed. For the rest of her life, she was going to remember that grisly image.

HE'D TOLD ABBY he was coming back to search the house. Instead he'd been standing in the hallway, unable to shake the grisly image of his friend's body from his mind—and unable to go back into the room where they'd found him in bed.

For days his feelings toward Oliver had been swinging wildly between anger and hope. Sometimes he'd pictured himself stomping into the house, grabbing the son of a bitch, and shaking him until his teeth rattled. He hadn't pictured anything like this.

Ollie might have taken some wild chances and pulled some harebrained stunts, but he'd always found a way out of the messes he'd gotten into.

Silently Steve admitted that he'd been counting on that. Counting on Ollie to help him figure out where Shannon was—and rescue her. One last crazy job together. And when they had gotten Shannon back, he would have made it very clear that if Oliver Gibbs ever put his family in danger again, he'd kill him. Only that wasn't going to be an option. Ollie was already dead.

All at once the loss hit him like a sledgehammer in the chest, and he doubled over. With one hand gripping the door frame, he tried to catch his breath.

Oliver Gibbs . . . dead. It was still almost impossible to believe.

Once the two of them had taken apart a brothel in Saigon looking for a girl who'd disappeared from her street on the way home from school. They'd found her and brought her back to her father, a tea merchant who'd been one of their earliest customers. Once they'd stood with their backs to a rough brick wall in Calcutta and fought off a street gang. Once Oliver had dragged him out of a burning nightclub in downtown Cairo.

They hadn't seen each other for more than a year. But he'd always known they were going to get together again, if only to chew over old times. And he'd known that if he were in a tight spot, he could call Ollie.

But not now. Never again.

He hadn't been prepared for the loss of Oliver Gibbs. Or, for that matter, any of the other nasty surprises life had thrown him over the past few weeks.

Now he was completely on his own. He'd thought things were bad when he'd left for India. In the past few minutes, the situation had deteriorated even further. His one lead to Amarjit Singh had died with Oliver.

In frustration, he socked his fist against the wall and came away with smarting knuckles.

The symbolism wasn't lost on him.

He and Ollie had done a lot of that—acting before they thought things through. In fact, living out here had been a little like one long adventure in never-never land. They'd thought of themselves as tough, macho guys. But really, neither one of them had been willing to grow up.

It had taken Abby to change him, Abby to make him realize what was really important in life. Abby's sweet persuasion to make him accept the risk of loving.

Abby. Oh, God. What if he couldn't keep her safe? What if he couldn't rescue their daughter?

His lips set in a grim line, he strode into the office and ripped open a desk drawer so hard that the contents scattered across the floor.

ABBY STOOD and walked toward the porch. She and Steve had come here to find out why the ILA had kidnapped their daughter, and they had less than a week to do it. Oliver Gibbs wasn't going to tell them a thing, and the only way they were going to figure out what he'd been up to was to work it out by themselves.

Abby stuffed the gun into her purse and made her way back up the steps. Somehow, once she'd stepped inside the door, it was easier to keep going. She could hear Steve down the hall, pulling open drawers and shuffling through papers. When she peered into the den, he whirled, his hand raised to fend off an attack—and she was reminded of the night before.

"I want to help. We can do it faster if we both look."

He didn't waste energy arguing but pointed to a couple of portable file drawers. "Okay. It looks as if he brought recent records here. You go through that stuff. I'll see if there's anything important in the bedroom."

Abby pulled open one of the drawers and found a jumble of papers stuffed haphazardly inside. It appeared as if Oliver simply used the file boxes to get the clutter out of the rest of the room. Was the whole house like that, with hidden storage areas in every corner? Sighing, she began to thumb through the mess. As she worked, she felt her anger building and knew she was using the mess as an outlet because the man was beyond her reach.

At the same time, she listened to Steve moving through the rest of the rooms. He was back in twenty minutes.

"Find anything?" she asked in a voice that was steadier than she'd expected.

"He didn't leave a note. Anything useful in his files?"

Abby handed him a piece of paper she'd laid on top of the desk. "This is more like a rat's nest than a filing system. But I got lucky."

Steve scanned the meager information, his face hardening. There was little more than a record of an agreement for the delivery of twenty-five units, a notation of payment, and three tiny initials in the corner. "So he did a job for the ILA six months ago." He glanced back at Abby. "Good work. I probably would have missed it."

"What does 'twenty-five units' mean?"

"Boxes of rifles? That's as good a guess as any."

She continued to go through the drawer while Steve shuffled through the contents of the desk.

"Got something." He straightened, smoothing out a crumpled sheet that was similar to the one Abby had found. This time, the payment notation was missing. But there was another set of initials after the ILA: *T.W.*

"So it looks as if you were right. He didn't get paid," Abby mused.

"Or he didn't live long enough to record it."

"But he crumpled the paper. Either he was careless with it, or he was angry."

Steve nodded.

Abby studied the notation. "Two units."

"Bigger weapons. Maybe they were buying mortars this time."

"What does 'T.W.' mean?"

He pursed his lips. "I'm not sure." Thoughtfully he smoothed out the paper and put it in his pocket.

Abby leaned back against the wall, feeling exhausted and dispirited. "We don't know much more than when we came!"

"There are a couple other things we can try. First, we'd better check out his warehouse."

They drove back down the hill to one of the corrugated metal buildings beside the airstrip. Steve took the key from its hiding place, and they went inside. Boxes were stacked against the far wall. Steve pried several open and removed the contents to see if all the layers were the same. They were, and he repacked them. They did contain weapons, but nothing a terrorist group couldn't have gotten relatively easily.

"I guess the good stuff isn't here," he remarked.

"Then where?"

"A hidey-hole. Like he had in Borneo."

Abby looked at him eagerly.

"This one's a ruined temple, with a nice dry storage area where the altar used to be. Nobody goes there because it's supposed to be under a curse. We had to check the house first, but I've been wondering all along if he might be camping out there."

Abby felt her energy level surge. "How far is it?"

"Not too far. And we can drive part of the way."

They climbed back into the Range Rover, and Steve drove up the hill again and around the house toward what looked like a tangle of underbrush. But he nosed the vehicle forward, plowing through a passage almost hidden from view. They came out on the other side into a lush canopy of foliage that reminded her of the place where they'd stopped for lunch, only more dense.

Ahead of them was a one-lane road leading off into the jungle. At first, Abby enjoyed the respite. But her mood changed as the lane narrowed and she began to feel the greenery pressing thickly in on either side as if it were getting ready to swallow them up. Leaves brushed against the window. Then a branch scraped like sharp fingernails across a blackboard, and she jumped. It broke off with a loud crack and fell beside the Rover as Steve moved forward.

Within minutes, the passage became too narrow for the vehicle to move forward. Steve pushed open his door into a tangle of vines that hung limply from several towering trees. Abby had trouble following suit.

"I guess you'll have to get out on my side," he suggested.

A few moments later, Abby was standing beside him on the rutted earth.

It was dark and quiet under the canopy of greenery. Unconsciously, Abby drew closer to Steve, and he slipped his arm around her shoulder. She stood looking around at the silent forest and shivered.

"What's wrong?"

"It's different," she whispered, realizing that her voice was the only thing that broke the unnatural stillness.

"From what?"

"From the place where we stopped for lunch. Don't you remember how alive it was? There were monkeys climbing around in the trees. And birds."

"Oliver went hunting out here. I guess the wildlife's cautious."

"Um," Abby murmured. But she still felt uneasy. This place was as silent as a cemetery. Instinctively, she reached for Steve's hand.

They started up the path. After a few dozen yards, she spotted a pile of large, dressed stones half hidden in the underbrush.

"There are some pretty interesting carvings," Steve told her. "Another time, I'll show you."

Abby looked from the stones to the surrounding vegetation. Some of it had turned yellow. Other plants had crumpled into brown heaps.

"How long since you've been here?" Abby asked.

"A couple of years, I guess."

"Were half the plants dead?"

Steve looked thoughtful. "I don't think so. But it was a different time of year. It's getting to be fall."

Abby scanned the underbrush. Other gray shapes lay among the wilting plants. More stones. And—

She stopped short, her eyes fixed on a crumpled, furry mass. "A dead monkey!"

"Where?"

She pointed, averting her face as she hurried past.

Several yards farther on, they spotted another little corpse. It was curled on its side much the way Oliver had been lying in his bed.

Abby's fingers dug into Steve's arm. Despite the heat, a shiver swept across her body.

"Come on."

"Wait!" She stood very still, not even breathing.

"What is it?"

"It's not just the animals. When we stopped for lunch, the jungle was full of insects buzzing and crawling. We had to cover our food, remember?"

"Yeah."

"Do you hear any now? See anything moving?"

They were both very quiet. Steve shook his head.

"And birds. I don't hear any birds."

He scanned the treetops, then studied the clumps of ruined vegetation around them.

"How far is the temple?" Abby asked.

"Just up the road."

He pointed, and she spotted the ravaged walls looming above the trees.

Abby felt goose bumps pepper her arms as she took in the ancient building—and the setting. Steve had told her people stayed away from this place because it was supposed to be cursed. Now it looked as if an ancient prophecy of evil had been fulfilled. In a ring around the walls, almost all of the foliage was dead or dying. The leaves closest to the crumbling edifice hung like dry chaff. A little farther away, the vegetation shaded into limp ochre. It was if the temple were the center of a giant bull's-eye done in shades of yellow, brown and gray.

"*Everything's* dead. Or dying," Abby whispered, taking a step back. "Was it like that before?"

"No."

"Then what's wrong now?"

Steve drew closer to her and wrapped a protective arm around her shoulders, as if that could shield her from the evil in the temple.

"What in the name of God did Oliver store there?" she questioned urgently.

"I don't know. But I'm getting you out of here." Steve grabbed Abby's hand and began to pull her back down the road. He didn't have to urge her to leave, but it was hard to move quickly. Her legs felt rubbery, and every breath seemed to burn her lungs, as if the atmosphere were permeated with acid.

Abby was breathing in shallow pants by the time they reached the vehicle. Quickly she crawled through the driver's door. Steve followed her inside, turned the key

in the ignition, and slammed the gear lever into re-
verse. Maneuvering backward up the narrow road was
awkward, and it took several minutes before they were
back at the spot where they'd entered.

Emerging into the sunlight was like coming up from
the pressure of the ocean depths. Steve swung the
Rover around and made for the house.

"Wh-where are we going?" Abby gasped.

"First we're putting some miles between us and that
place. Maybe Oliver shot himself because he was sick
and knew he wasn't going to get well. Or maybe the
stuff back there did something to his mind."

Abby nodded tightly. "Do you think it's chemical
weapons?"

"Maybe. Or biological." He slammed his hands
against the steering wheel. "I wonder if he had any idea
what he was carrying." Suddenly he turned to Abby.
"Do you feel okay?"

She sat very still in the seat. Her skin was covered
with a fine sheen of perspiration. Her heart was
pounding. And her breath was still ragged. "I have a
headache. A tension headache, I think. What about
you?"

"Nothing special."

Just a tension headache, she repeated silently. But
she couldn't dispel the nagging fear at the edge of her
mind. "How long were we there?"

"After we started seeing the dead monkeys? Maybe
twenty minutes."

"I think a doctor ought to check us over. And...and
I think the people around here ought to be warned to
stay away from the area."

"Yeah."

As the Rover sped along, Abby slumped in her seat,
sick and shaky, and wishing she could filter out her

nervous reaction so she could judge the real state of her health. They'd been exposed to *something*, but only briefly. They didn't know when Oliver had picked up his cargo, so he might have been in contact with the stuff for weeks or months. The same was true for the jungle around the temple. How long would it have taken for the monkeys to die and the vegetation to turn brown? What was a safe level of exposure? A safe distance away for humans? Would she and Steve start coming down with symptoms in a little while? Or had they escaped infection?

Steve reached over and stroked his hand against her cheek. She turned her face and pressed her lips against his knuckles.

"I wish I'd left you at the hotel."

"I'm glad you didn't. But I'll feel better when we find out what's in the temple," she murmured. "Can we assume it's whatever weapons Oliver shipped for the ILA?"

Steve shook his head. "I wish to hell we could. But if he was stupid enough to get in the arms business, it could be something for another customer."

"We've got to find out what it is and how to handle it."

"I wonder if I can get a decontamination suit in Delhi," he mused.

"What do you know about decontamination suits?"

"Not much. Just that they exist."

"Steve, you're not going in there until we make sure it's safe."

"Somebody has to—"

Abby swung toward him, her fingers clamping down on his shoulder. The vehicle swerved, and he eased up on the accelerator.

"Steve, Oliver is *dead. The jungle around that temple is dead.* It was one thing for us to innocently start up that road. But now we know exposure to that place is toxic. If you're thinking about risking your life, remember that it's not going to help Shannon."

He sighed. "You're right."

Abby slowly let out the knife-sharp breath she'd been holding. "Maybe the first thing we ought to think about is an autopsy of Oliver's body, to see if there are any poisons or bacterial agents in his system."

"Yeah." Steve's eyes narrowed as he squinted into the sunset.

"Now what are you thinking?"

He sighed again. "That we have a very sticky problem here. It looks like we've got a public health hazard in the jungle. But if the ILA's stuff is stored in the temple, we can't take a chance on having the authorities clear out the place. If they confiscate the contents they'll probably destroy them. That would be putting Shannon's life in jeopardy."

"So what do we do?" Abby's question came out high and reedy.

"There's a doctor in town about twenty-five kilometers from here. Dr. Raj Sunduram. He treated Oliver for a gunshot wound once without reporting it to the authorities."

"Why?"

"Money, for one thing. A lot of the people around here are very poor, and he takes care of their medical needs for free. Which means he's chronically short of cash. But I think he's also got a sense of adventure. He used to ask us to stop by and spend the evening so he could hear about our more colorful exploits."

Abby was intrigued by Steve's description of the man, but she knit her fingers together in her lap as she considered asking for Dr. Sunduram's help. She hadn't bargained on putting anyone else's life in danger. And that wasn't the only stumbling block.

"How well do you know him? I mean, what will he do for money? Will he betray us for a price?"

Steve looked thoughtful. "You're right. Trusting him is taking a risk. But from what I know about him, I think he'll be more likely to help if we tell him everything."

"You mean about Shannon?"

"Yeah."

"Oh, Steve. The note said—"

"I know." He cut her off. "Unfortunately, this is something we can't handle alone. We've got to trust *someone*."

Abby nodded. But as the last rays of the sun glinted off the windshield, she sat rigidly in her seat—trying to picture Raj Sunduram, trying to figure out how he'd react to Steve Claiborne and his wife appearing out of nowhere with a desperate problem.

ABBY STOOD several feet behind Steve, arms clenched at her sides, as he knocked on the doctor's door. During the forty-minute drive, she'd grabbed for a familiar image and imagined the physician would look a little like Omar Sharif. As he stood in the open doorway she saw that only his eyes resembled the actor's.

In reality, he was a short, balding man with a round face and dark, liquid eyes fringed by dark lashes. Steve had told her he'd gotten his medical training in Scotland. As he ushered them into the white stucco house, Abby found that his British-Indian accent was tinged with the faintest hint of a brogue. If they'd been in the living room of their Baltimore home, the combination would have amused her.

He shook hands with her warmly, yet his gaze was appraising. Then he turned back to Steve. "I'd like to think you flew here from America to surprise an old friend. But I have the feeling you've come to me with a problem," he said.

"Yes," Abby answered.

"Well, then, come in. Sit down and be comfortable. Luckily, I'm not seeing patients this evening," he said as he ushered them into a cluttered roomful of carved chests, brass tables, and overstuffed sofas and chairs. The chests and tables would have fetched a fortune in a Howard Street antique shop. The upholstered pieces looked like flea market castoffs.

Abby sank onto one of the sofas. The ancient cushions were lumpy, but not uncomfortable.

"So what can I do for you?" Dr. Sunduram inquired as he took a seat opposite.

Steve gave Abby a quick look, and she nodded. In a clipped voice, he began a concise explanation of what had happened over the past week, and she realized he must have been silently preparing what he was going to say while he was driving. When he'd finished, the physician's expression was unreadable. "What do you want from me?"

Abby tried to swallow and found her throat was too dry. Steve got up, paced to the window, and turned around. "For starters, it would help if you could tell us about the state of Oliver's health when he took his life. When was the last time you saw him?"

"I'm sorry. It's been at least three months. I was starting to wonder if he'd gone out of town. I take it you think he may have been exposed to whatever is in the temple?"

"Yes."

"We may have been, also," Abby broke in. "And it could be contagious. If you want us to leave, just say so. But . . . but I'd appreciate your not telling the authorities about Shannon."

"I'm not planning to send you away—or put your daughter's life in jeopardy," he answered mildly. "I was just thinking about the best way to have the body brought here so I can give you some answers."

"I'm sorry," Abby murmured. "I'm—"

"Worried about your daughter," he finished for her. "And your own health."

Abby nodded.

He gave her a sympathetic look, and she was suddenly conscious of how she must appear. Pale. Drawn. Disheveled.

He rose from his chair. "Come along to the surgery. I'd better give both of you a physical examination, although I won't be able to tell you much until I do some lab work."

"I understand," Abby said as she followed him down the hall to another wing of the house. They passed through a waiting area and half a dozen examination cubicles.

Abby winced as he began to listen to her heart.

"Do your breasts hurt?"

"Yes."

"It would be easier for you if you let your milk supply dry up."

"I know, but I'm going to nurse Shannon again. When we get her back," she said fiercely.

"You have shown a lot of courage, making the trip out here."

"I couldn't sit at home—not knowing. And . . . and I needed to be with Steve."

The physician nodded as he began to examine Abby's eyes and ears. Then he tested her reflexes.

"Well, everything checks out normally so far," he reported a few minutes later.

Some of the tension went out of Abby's shoulders.

After taking a blood sample, Dr. Sunduram opened the door. "Steve, we're ready for you now."

There was no answer.

"Steve?" Abby called. After several tense seconds of silence, she slid down from the table, pushed past the doctor, and ran toward the room where they'd been sitting.

It was empty.

"Steve? Where are you?" she called again. With a frisson of panic, she looked out the window toward the spot where they had parked. The Range Rover was missing, too.

Irrationally, Abby threw open the door and rushed outside into the twilight. But the vehicle was definitely gone. There wasn't even a cloud of dust lingering in the rutted access road.

"STEVE LEFT US A NOTE." Raj Sunduram held out a lined sheet obviously torn from a small notebook.

Snatching the paper from the physician's hand, she moved back into the light and scanned the hastily scrawled words. "He's gone back to Oliver's house to do a more thorough search," she repeated aloud, and then crumpled the sheet in her balled fist.

"Come and sit down, Mrs. Claiborne. Steve will be back as soon as he finishes."

"Do you have a car? Can you drive me there?"

"Steve didn't wish you to go with him."

"But—"

"Please. Be logical. Your husband left you here because he wants to keep you safe."

Abby stood for several more moments, staring out the door and down the road. She'd asked Steve not to do anything foolish. He'd gone off to do just that—as soon as he'd found a good place to leave her. Anger welled up inside her. Anger mixed with equal parts fear. Yet she knew the doctor was right. Steve had put himself in jeopardy, which meant she couldn't. Her shoulders slumped as she turned.

"Let me see what the cook left for dinner."

"I can't eat."

"Your body is expending large amounts of energy producing milk. If you don't want to make yourself sick, you must eat."

The words brought a tight feeling to Abby's breasts. She knew the doctor was right, but she didn't know how she was going to choke anything down.

He led her along a hallway toward a kitchen that looked like a set for a 1940's movie and pulled out a chair at a Formica-topped table.

"Do you drink *lassi?*"

Abby nodded. A glass of the sweetened yogurt drink appeared in front of her. She sipped it slowly, hardly tasting the tart flavor. It was the same with the vegetarian dishes Sunduram brought to the table. They could have been made of straw for all Abby cared. But she did manage to swallow some of the food.

"It might help you to talk about the things that are troubling you," the doctor observed after Abby had declined a cup of cardamom-flavored tea.

She gave him a half smile. "That's usually my line."

"Oh?"

"I'm a psychologist. I try to get my patients to talk about what's bothering them."

He smiled back. "Because you know the benefits."

She closed her eyes for a moment, thinking of what she might say to this stranger who had put her at ease so quickly.

Then the truth came tumbling out. The truth she hadn't quite dared articulate—even to herself. "It's not just Shannon. It's everything. God, I was feeling so smug about my life, so safe and secure. I'd gotten everything I always wanted. Marriage to the man I loved. A baby on the way. My career." She gulped. "Only it's all blown up in my face. And I—I can't handle it."

"Who could?"

"I'm not just frightened for my daughter," she whispered. "That would be bad enough. But I'm frightened for me and Steve, too. We met right after his sister died, when he came back to Baltimore to find out what had happened to her. I fell in love with him then. But taking the chance of loving someone was a big risk for him."

"Yes. I remember what he was like. He's changed a lot. And you're obviously responsible."

"I knew being married to him wouldn't be easy. But, God, I never thought our relationship would be under this much stress! This is the kind of crisis that tears husbands and wives apart."

"Or it reinforces the bond between them."

"The stress didn't start with the kidnapping. Shannon was born eight weeks early. I was so worried about my baby that I spent almost every waking moment at the hospital. And while I was wrapped up with Shannon, I wasn't thinking about much of anything else." It was several seconds before she continued. "The doctor told me we could bring Shannon home, and I knew I had another chance to make things work out right for the three of us. Then . . . then we got to the hospital, and Shannon wasn't in her little bed.''

''She was snatched away from you when you were already at your most vulnerable.''

Abby had been staring over the doctor's right shoulder. She brought her eyes back to his. ''I hadn't thought about it like that.''

''No, you don't have enough perspective to see how courageous you are.''

''I—I'm just trying to get my daughter back!''

''Yes. So here you are halfway around the world. In a village in the back of beyond, and—''

The sound of an engine outside made Abby jump up before the doctor could finish his sentence. She was down the hall and heading for the front door when it opened and Steve stepped into the light. His gray pallor made her stop in her tracks.

''What? What's wrong?''

''I found some papers taped to the bottom of a desk drawer. I know who Oliver Gibbs was working for on the ILA deal.''

Chapter Eight

The harsh sound of Steve's voice and the grim look on his face made Abby's throat constrict so tightly that she could barely speak. "Satan?"

Steve laughed acidly. "It might as well be. Except in this life, he's an international arms dealer named Tang Wu. He'll sell anything to anyone—including the ILA—as long as the price is right."

"Are you sure it's him?"

"Remember the letters T.W. that were on that record sheet you found in Oliver's files?"

"You didn't know what they meant," Abby countered.

"Yeah, well, I kept whacking my brain because I knew I'd seen them before somewhere. Then, when I was waiting for you to finish up in the exam room, Wu's name popped into my head. So I went back to look for more evidence—and found it where Oliver had hidden it." Steve pulled several folded sheets of paper from his shirt pocket. "We'd talked about Wu because Ollie wanted to accept a shipment from him once before."

"And you vetoed the idea," Abby guessed.

Steve nodded. "Wu is the kind of guy who will take your money and then leave you twisting in the wind if he thinks he can get away with it. I didn't like him. I didn't like his methods. And I didn't like what he was selling.''

"But after you left, Oliver went ahead and contacted him," Abby murmured.

"Or Wu knew I was gone and decided to take another crack at Gibbs."

"Could . . . could Wu have come back here to get his shipment, killed Oliver, and made it look like a suicide?"

"I'll be able to give you a professional opinion on that when I see the body," Sunduram interjected. "However, from what Steve says, if Wu or his men have been here, then he wouldn't have left without the merchandise, whatever it is."

Steve didn't answer him.

Abby felt the blood freeze in her veins. "But . . . then . . . Shannon—" She swayed toward her husband, and he opened his arms. A shudder went through her slender frame as she pressed her face blindly against his shirtfront.

Steve held her close, yet he murmured no words of comfort, and his posture remained rigid.

"What?" Abby questioned urgently. "What are you thinking?"

"That we still can't risk going into the temple. I was talking about decontamination suits earlier, but I guess you've got to have *some* idea of what you're protecting yourself against."

Abby pulled away from Steve, her eyes fierce. "The only way we're going to find out what Oliver was transporting and whether it's still missing is to ask Wu. Where is he?"

"Hong Kong."

"How long does it take to get there?"

"Abby, you don't know what we'd be getting into. Talking to Wu isn't a matter of going up and knocking on his door. The man has enemies. He lives in a fortress and has a private army guarding him. You don't get close to him without a gilt-edged invitation and a security check."

"It doesn't matter what kind of defenses he's got. We have to go after him. There has to be a weak link somewhere in his defense."

Her husband's fingers dug into her flesh. "*We* don't have to."

Abby shook her head. "No, Steve. From what you said, you can't get to him by yourself, because brute force won't work, or stealth, for that matter. We've got to research him, find out what his weaknesses are. What would lure him out of his fortress."

Dr. Sunduram had come up beside them. "I think she's right," he said quietly.

Abby gave him a grateful look. Steve scowled.

"You don't have to settle anything right now, and whatever you decide, you're certainly not going to fly to Hong Kong tonight. Both of you need a good night's sleep." The doctor sighed. "I'm sorry. I've never encountered this kind of situation before, and I'm thinking of things as we go along. It's probably wise to discard the clothes you were wearing in the jungle."

Abby looked down at her wrinkled skirt and blouse.

"Just as a precaution," he continued. "I'd also suggest a good scrub under running water. Come along and let me show you the bathroom and my guest room."

Steve brought their luggage into the house. While the two men continued to talk in the sitting room, Abby undressed and left her clothes in the hall. Then she stood for a long time under the ancient shower head, scrubbing her hair and then her skin. Automatically, she began to express the milk from her breasts. Then, with a choked little sound in her throat, she stopped. There was something else she hadn't considered.

She'd been clinging to the idea of nursing Shannon when they got her back. She couldn't do that now. Not when she didn't know if she'd absorbed some kind of deadly chemical. If it was in her tissues, she'd be giving her daughter tainted milk. And an infant's tolerance for the poison would be far less than an adult's.

Head bent, Abby stood for a long moment with the water pounding down on her scalp. Tears began to leak from between her closed eyelids. She felt as if pieces of herself were being torn away, one terrible loss after another. And now this.

A knock at the door brought her back to the here and now.

"Abby? Are you okay?" Steve's voice was muffled by the barrier and the running water, but she couldn't mistake its edge of worry. Her body snapped erect. How long had she been standing under the water like a zombie?

"Abby?"

"Yes," she managed. "I'm sorry I'm taking so long. I'll be right out."

"It's okay. I was just concerned about you."

After wiping the tears away with the back of her hand, she turned off the water, stepped out of the shower, and reached for the towel Dr. Sunduram had given her.

The men were down the hall talking again. Instead of joining them, Abby went into the guest bedroom, slipped between the sheets and lay her head wearily against the pillow. She hadn't thought she could sleep, but she was too tired to wait for Steve. Within minutes, blessed oblivion swallowed her.

ABBY WOKE EARLY—alone. A moment of panic seized her. Then she heard low voices drifting down the hall. Steve. And Dr. Sunduram.

As soon as she stepped into the kitchen and saw the expression on her husband's face, she felt the world tilt and grabbed the back of a chair for support. "Shannon! Something's happened to Shannon."

Steve was on his feet, surging toward her. "No! I talked to Jason this morning. She's all right."

"But?"

"Singh's sent us a lock of her hair to let us know she's arrived safely."

The air *whooshed* out of Abby's chest and she sagged against Steve. When she could speak again, she managed, "He didn't just send the hair. He sent a note, too, didn't he?"

"It wasn't anything we don't already know."

"Damn it, tell me!"

Steve sighed. "It was a reminder that we have less than a week to get his merchandise back."

"Oh, God."

Her knees gave way, and Steve lowered her into the chair. Then he hunkered down beside her. "Jason said he'd been expecting something like that," he said.

"Why?"

"Because he's had experience with kidnappers. He says that's the way they operate. They *want* you on edge and upset. They *want* you to be afraid of what will happen if you don't meet their demands. And they want to tantalize you—to send you a reminder of what you have to lose."

The words penetrated the fear that had gathered in Abby's middle, and she sat up straighter. Jason was right. Amarjit Singh was trying to play with their minds. Steve must have sensed the change in her. He squeezed her arm, and she gave him a half smile. "I'm not going to fall apart."

He nodded, and she saw how worried he'd been about her reaction.

To show him she was in control, she picked up another topic. "Have you been discussing the temple?" she said.

"Yeah. Raj is going to spread the word among the villagers to stay away from that area," Steve told her.

Abby looked at Dr. Sunduram. "Thank you. I was afraid that someone might get sick." She swallowed. "Or die, even, if they went poking around there."

"As Steve told you, the building is already a place to be avoided. It's only a matter of reinforcing that interdiction. The people are accustomed to heeding me in matters of health."

Steve poured Abby a cup of spicy tea and then pushed in his own chair. "I'm going to pack while you eat. Then we'd better get going."

"All right."

After Steve had left, Dr. Sunduram cleared his throat. "I've been doing some more thinking. I know you have a lot on your plate. But speaking of health matters, you mentioned you were planning to nurse your baby again."

Abby's fingers tightened on the handle of her cup. "I—I reconsidered that last night. Since we don't know what might be in the temple, and how much exposure we could have gotten."

"It was probably minimal. But you do need to err on the side of conservatism, as far as an infant is concerned."

"I understand that."

"You're going to be uncomfortable for a couple of days."

Abby rolled her shoulders. "Yes."

"But that will pass. A woman's body stops producing milk very quickly when it isn't being removed regularly."

"Thank you for telling me."

Dr. Sunduram reached across the table and covered Abby's hand. "Bring Shannon to visit me when you get her back."

Up until that moment, Abby had thought she was handling her emotions. Suddenly tears blurred her vision, and she struggled to contain them. "I will," she whispered, unable to look into the doctor's eyes.

"Forgive me. I wasn't thinking—"

"No. It's not your fault." Scraping back her chair, Abby scrambled up and fled the kitchen. After escaping through the front door, she stood in the small garden, dragging in gulps of the cool morning air.

She didn't see the flowers or the backdrop of hills. In her mind, she saw Shannon stretching out a hand toward her pleadingly. Then, as she watched, the tiny face puckered and grew red, and the baby began to cry.

"Shannon," Abby murmured, unconsciously wrapping her arms around herself. "Oh, Shannon. Don't cry. Mommy's going to come and get you." But the infant's sobs increased.

Could her baby sense the terrible danger she was in? Or was she simply hungry? Wet? Sick? Abby unconsciously hugged herself as she anxiously studied the

PLAY THIS

MATCH GAME 3

for big money prizes—you could
WIN UP TO $1-MILLION!
get Free Books and Surprise Gift, too

MATCH 3 you are instantly eligible to WIN $10,000	STICK 1st MATCH HERE	STICK 2nd MATCH HERE	STICK 3rd MATCH HERE
MATCH 3 you are instantly eligible to WIN $35,000	STICK 1st MATCH HERE	STICK 2nd MATCH HERE	STICK 3rd MATCH HERE
MATCH 3 you are instantly eligible to WIN $1-MILLION	STICK 1st MATCH HERE	STICK 2nd MATCH HERE	STICK 3rd MATCH HERE
MATCH 3 and get FOUR FREE BOOKS	STICK 1st MATCH HERE	STICK 2nd MATCH HERE	STICK 3rd MATCH HERE
MATCH 3 and get A GREAT SURPRISE GIFT	STICK 1st MATCH HERE	STICK 2nd MATCH HERE	STICK 3rd MATCH HERE

CAREFULLY PRE-FOLD, TEAR ALONG DOTTED LINES, COMPLETE "MATCH 3" GAME & RETURN IN REPLY ENVELOPE PROVIDED

▲ FOLD, REMOVE THIS BOTTOM PART, RETURN "MATCH 3" GAME PIECE ▲

THIS COULD BE THE LUCKIEST DAY OF YOUR LIFE

because your "MATCH 3" Game qualifies you for a chance to win Big Money Prizes—up to $1-MILLION in Lifetime Cash—for FREE! It's also your chance to get Free Books & an Exciting Free Surprise Gift with no obligation to buy anything, now or ever. Just find all the matching stamps you can, stick them on your Game, fill in your name & address on the other side & return your Game in the reply envelope provided. We'll take care of the rest!

HERE'S HOW TO PLAY

"MATCH 3"

1 Detach this, your "MATCH 3" Game, & the page of stamps enclosed. Look for matching symbols among the stamps & stick all you find on your "MATCH 3" Game.

2 Successfully complete rows 1 through 3 & you will instantly & auto-matically be qualified for a chance to win All Big Money Prizes—up to a MILLION-$$$ in Lifetime Income($33,333.33 each year for 30 years). (SEE RULES, BACK OF BOOK, FOR FULL PARTICULARS.)

3 Successfully complete row 4 & we will send you 4 brand-new HARLEQUIN Intrigue® novels—for FREE! These Free Books have a cover price of $2.99 each, but they are yours to keep absolutely free. There's no catch. You're under no obligation to buy anything. We charge nothing—Zero—for your first shipment. And you don't have to make any minimum number of purchases—not even one!

4 The fact is thousands of Readers enjoy receiving books by mail from the Harlequin Reader Service®. They like the convenience of home delivery...they like getting the best new novels...and they love our discount prices!

5 Successfully complete row 5 &, in addition to the Free Books, we will also send you a very nice Free Surprise Gift, as extra thanks for trying our Reader Service.

6 Play the "Lucky Stars" & "Dream Car Tiebreaker" Games also enclosed & you could WIN AGAIN & AGAIN because these are Bonus Prizes, all for one winner, & on top of any Cash Prize you may win!

YES! I've completed my "MATCH 3" Game. Send me any Big Money Prize to which I am entitled just as soon as winners are determined. Also send me the Free Books & Free Surprise Gift under the no-obligation-to-buy-ever terms explained above and on the back of the stamps & reply. (No purchase necessary as explained below.)

181 CIH AJDC
(U-H-I-07/93)

Name _____

Street Address _____ Apt. # _____

City _____ State _____ Zip Code _____

© 1991 HARLEQUIN ENTERPRISES LTD.

small, delicate face that had stolen into her mind, trying to determine how Shannon was faring.

Then she shook her head. She wasn't really observing her daughter, was she? She was only imagining Shannon as she'd seen her lying in her isolette at the hospital. Yet she couldn't shake the conviction that she was somehow spying on the enemy camp. And that there was some invisible bond connecting her to her baby. It didn't make any logical sense, but it made her feel better.

"Did you finish eating already?"

Abby jumped. She hadn't even heard Steve come out. She sensed him studying her profile. "I—I'm anxious to get going."

"Yeah."

Raj Sunduram opened the door, and Abby felt his sympathetic eyes on her, but this time he kept his words neutral. "My nurse will be wondering why I'm not in the office, so I'd better say goodbye to you now."

"You've been so good to us," Abby told him. "You could have said you didn't want to get involved, and I would have understood."

"I have a habit of 'getting involved,' as you put it."

"I can't thank you enough for everything."

After a moment of hesitation, he hugged her gently. "Good luck. And take care."

"We will."

The two men shook hands, and then Abby and Steve were off.

"He's a good friend," Abby said, looking back toward the house.

"I didn't know how good until last night. I tried to give him some money. He wouldn't take it."

She was afraid she'd start to cry again if she mentioned the doctor's request that they return with Shan-

non, so they rode in silence for several miles. Abby
stared blindly out the window. The rules kept changing. That was the worst part. Just as she and Steve
thought they had everything figured out, the whole
pattern would shift, and it would seem as if they were
farther from finding their daughter than they had been
only hours before.

She needed to feel in control of *something*. So did
Steve. Over and above their fears for Shannon, the lack
of control made everything so much worse.

"Let's not waste the drive. What can you tell me
about Tang Wu?" Abby finally asked. "How old is he?
What does he look like?"

"Jason's going to have a briefing folder waiting for
us in Hong Kong."

"Tell me what you know."

"Okay. He's in his late forties, I'd guess, from the
length of time he's been prominent in the world arms
market. But he looks younger. No gray in his hair.
Probably he dyes it."

"He's vain," Abby said.

"I guess I didn't think about it that way. But you're
right."

For the next several hours, Abby quizzed Steve, and
he did his best to supply her with information. Then,
as they approached the city, he needed to concentrate
on the route to the airport.

Abby had arrived in India on a commercial airliner.
Steve had flown the Learjet Jason's contact had provided. He'd already called ahead to the terminal, so
making arrangements to take off took a relatively short
time.

Abby had never gone in for the jet-setting life-style
of some of her parents' friends, but this was one time
when she could appreciate the concept of flitting

around the world at will. Still, even with a fast plane, it was a seven-hour trip from New Delhi to Hong Kong, with a stop in Bangkok for refueling.

THEY ARRIVED in the early evening. On the taxi ride from the airport, Steve leaned back wearily against the seat.

"I know you must be beat," Abby sympathized. "It's been a long day." She'd been able to nap during part of the flight. Steve had driven the car and then piloted the plane.

"I'll be okay."

"As soon as we settle into our room, you can get some sleep."

"We'll see."

Instead of pressing him, Abby looked out the window at the unfamiliar Hong Kong landscape glowing richly in the red rays of the setting sun. New Delhi was a crowded, bustling city, but it was spread out over mile after mile of cheap land. Hong Kong was confined to a small island off the coast of mainland China. There was nowhere to build but up, so huge, modern, office and apartment buildings crowded in upon each other with hardly a break in the skyline. Abby could picture the island sinking under their weight.

Their hotel overlooked the harbor. Steve flopped onto the bed of their spacious suite and glanced at her apologetically. "You're sure you don't mind if I get a little sleep?"

"I wish you would."

"What about you?"

"I'm too keyed up." She gestured toward the thick folder they'd picked up at the desk. "I'll look over the materials on Wu and mark anything that I think is interesting."

"Okay."

"Why don't you take a shower first? You'll be more comfortable."

"Yeah."

And you haven't eaten, either, she thought as he disappeared behind the closed door.

When he emerged from the bathroom twenty minutes later wearing a snow-white, terry-cloth robe provided by the hotel, Abby had ordered tea and sandwiches from room service.

"Thanks," he said, picking up a triangle from the plate on the table. He finished it in a few bites and then ate the second.

She saw his eyes go from the cup of tea in her hand to her breasts, and the pressure she'd been trying to ignore turned into pain.

"You've, uh, switched from milk to tea," he said, his voice husky.

"Um."

"Raj and I were talking in the morning. Did he tell you it might not be a good idea to nurse Shannon?"

"I'd already decided."

"Abby, I'm sorry. I know how much you wanted to."

She fought the tears gathering behind her eyes. The last tie to her daughter. Cut.

Steve's hand covered hers, and she turned her face into his shoulder. Neither one of them went back to the meal.

Finally she reached for the confidential dossier on Wu.

"Are you sure you don't want me to help you go through the material?" Steve asked.

Abby looked at the deeply etched circles under his eyes, afraid he might insist on staying up. "No. You'll do a better job after you've gotten some rest."

As he headed back to the bedroom, Abby settled down on the sofa to learn everything she could about Tang Wu.

Someone in the U.S. intelligence service must have been collecting information on him for years, because Abby found an exhaustive account of his life—complete with details that could only have come from close observation. The written material was accompanied by a set of photographs that chronicled the man through the years.

Tang Wu's father had been an associate of Nationalist Chinese leader Chiang Kai-shek as far back as his exile in Szechwan during the Japanese invasion in 1937. The family spent World War II in Chungking, where Tang was born in 1948. But with the Communist takeover of the country in 1949, the Wu family fled with other Nationalists to Taiwan.

Tang had used his natural skills as a linguist to get a job with the foreign ministry, where he made contact with government and military leaders from around the world. While still working for the government, he began arranging arms deals, first with surplus World War II materials. But as the demand for more sophisticated weapons increased, he found new sources of supply—often among U.S. manufacturers.

By the late seventies, when he resigned from the Nationalist Chinese foreign ministry, he was well established in Hong Kong as one of the world's chief arms brokers.

For three hours, Abby read steadily through the dossier, feeling less and less optimistic the more she learned about the man's security arrangements. Steve was right. Wu's estate on the outskirts of town was guarded by what amounted to a private army.

Doggedly, she went on to the more personal material, searching for signs that a man like Wu would respond to a heartfelt plea from a mother who wanted her daughter back.

The more she read, however, the more she doubted that an appeal for compassion would work. Wu's relationship with his wife had been cold. In fact, he seemed to harbor the traditional Chinese attitude toward women. He would see an infant daughter as of little value—except as a future pawn in a marriage alliance.

When she got to the last section of the report, she wondered who had provided the information, since the text was replete with all sorts of personal data that would only be known to one of Wu's intimates—or a servant. Abby found out which brand of tooth gel the man used, which cigars he liked, his favorite foods, and the fact that he considered the diamond ring he'd inherited from his grandfather a special good luck charm. There was also information on his sexual proclivities.

The latter material reminded her of case studies she'd run across in abnormal psychology books. As she read, she unconsciously wrinkled her nose as if an unpleasant odor were slowly seeping under the door.

A suggestion of movement from across the room made her eyes flick away from the page. Steve was studying her from the bedroom doorway. She studied him back. The hotel robe was the same, but now he looked rested.

"That's quite an expression on your face," he commented.

She pursed her lips. "I'm afraid I don't like Mr. Wu very much."

"I gather."

Abby rolled her shoulders, regretting that she'd been sitting in the same position for hours.

"Have you been working all this time?"

"Yes."

He came over, sat down beside her and closed the folder that lay open in her lap. "Why don't we trade places. You sleep, and I'll catch up on the reading."

As soon as Steve made the suggestion, Abby realized how weary she was. At the same time, she was bursting to share her new insights. "I have an idea about how to get to Wu," she ventured.

Steve picked up the folder and laid it on the coffee table. "Let me read the material first. Then I'll be able to comment."

Abby dragged in a deep breath and let it out slowly. She knew he was right. What she was going to propose would sound too outrageous—if Steve hadn't read the dossier.

Chapter Nine

"Did you finish the dossier?" Abby asked as they sat eating breakfast the next morning.

"Yeah."

"Then I guess we'd better talk about Tang Wu."

"I've been speculating on what you're going to say."

"Oh?"

"You think you know when Wu is most vulnerable. And you have some scheme for getting close to him."

Abby's teacup clattered against the saucer. "He's most vulnerable when he's visiting the fancy bordellos that cater to his sexual tastes. He's relaxed. He's had a few drinks. And he leaves his guards outside. He's not expecting trouble."

Steve nodded. "The place is owned by a woman who calls herself Madame Pearl. I know her."

"You do?" Abby leaned forward, suddenly curious. "How well do you know her?"

"She was a client of mine a few years ago, not the other way around."

"What did you do for her?"

"Brought in cases of alcoholic beverages and fancy gourmet items that are expensive to buy here. Pearl likes to be known for her lavish hospitality as much as her sexual services."

"How often did you help her out?"

Steve shrugged. "I had a standing order, and I filled it whenever I flew into Hong Kong. But, of course, I haven't seen her since I came back to Baltimore."

"You parted on good terms?"

"Yes. I guess she even owes me a couple of favors."

"So would she tell you when Wu is expected? Better yet, would she contact him and tell him she has a new girl she knows he'll like?"

Steve looked thoughtful. "She might. But what happens afterward? When Wu figures out she set him up? What keeps him from going after her?"

Abby was prepared for the question. "He's vain, remember? And the Asian concept of saving face is deeply ingrained in his makeup. Not only that, if he wants to stay in a business where he's selling his contacts as much as anything else, he has to protect his reputation. He won't tell anyone he walked into a trap. And you can make it clear that if he takes any kind of revenge on Madame Pearl, you'll let every one of his clients know why."

Steve set down his fork. "Okay. I'll concede those points. But I'm not going to let you use yourself as bait. That's what you have in mind, isn't it?"

Abby flushed.

"You think I'm going to let you go upstairs alone in a brothel with a man like Tang Wu?"

"You'll follow us. You'll come in before anything happens."

She saw him swallow and went on quickly before he could fix the picture of her and Wu alone in a bedroom firmly in his mind. "I know you're thinking that we could use a woman who already works there to act as lure. But it would have to be somebody new— someone he hadn't seen. And more than that, it would

have to be a woman who won't give anything away by
her facial expression. You can't count on a prostitute
to maintain the deception that everything is perfectly
normal. You can count on me."

"Oh, yeah, right. Normal for whom?"

"You know what I mean. I'm a trained psychologist. I don't give my private thoughts away to my patients. And that's what he'll be like to me. Only I'm not
going to give him the kind of treatment he's anticipating."

"You gave your thoughts away to me when you were
reading about him," Steve shot back.

"Because I wasn't trying to guard them. I didn't realize you were standing in the bedroom doorway looking at me." Abby sighed. "Steve, stop arguing with me.
You know we're going to end up doing it this way, because we don't have any choice."

His sigh matched hers.

"Call Madame Pearl and tell her you're back in
town—and that you want to bring someone over to
meet her."

"What about Amarjit's warning to keep our dealings secret?"

"I don't think the Lion of Punjab and the Tart
Queen of Hong Kong move in the same circles."

Steve laughed. "I'll bet you've been waiting for
hours to deliver that line."

"Yeah."

He shook his head and reached for the telephone.

"You still remember Madame Pearl's number?"
Abby asked.

"No. But I have a contact in town who will know it."

"IT'S GOOD TO SEE YOU again, Steve," Madame Pearl said as she swept into the tastefully furnished living room of her establishment.

She was tall, thin, well-dressed and elegant-looking—probably of Eurasian heritage, Abby decided as they eyed each other cautiously.

"Yes. And I'd like you to meet my wife."

"Ah. It's seldom that I meet a man's wife."

"We have a rather complicated problem," Steve began.

"Don't be shy about confiding in me. There's nothing I haven't heard before, and almost nothing that we can't arrange here." Madame Pearl smiled encouragingly as she took a seat opposite them.

Abby glanced at Steve's flushed face and saw that he wasn't sure how to respond, so she jumped into the conversation. "I know that you've seen and heard almost everything, but maybe there are still some things that shock you. Would you be shocked to hear that our baby was stolen from the hospital six days ago and is being held by East Indian rebels? Or that we have less than six days left in which to pay the ransom? After that, they're going to kill our daughter—our only child—unless we give them what they want."

Abby saw the stunned look in Madame Pearl's eyes and went on quickly. "The rebels aren't holding us up for money. It would be easy if they were, because we'd pay anything they asked to get Shannon back." Abby's voice cracked, and she had to pause for several seconds. "What they want is a weapon Steve's former partner, Oliver Gibbs, was supposed to deliver to them. They couldn't threaten Oliver because he's dead. Which also means he can't give us any advice. So there's only one place we can turn for information—to the man who arranged the sale, Tang Wu. You know him, so you can imagine how much he's going to care about saving our daughter.''

For long moments the woman said nothing, and Abby could feel her heart thumping inside her chest. She half wished she hadn't spilled her heart out like that, hadn't given so much away.

Then Madame Pearl raised her eyes. Their expression pierced all the way to Abby's soul.

''I had a daughter,'' the older woman said. ''Her father didn't think I was a fit person to raise her, so he took her away from me. I haven't seen her in twenty years.''

''Oh. I'm so sorry.''

''No one in this city knows I was ever a mother.''

A look of understanding passed between the two women. Abby caught her breath. Madame Pearl empathized with her. But that didn't mean she would go along with their plans.

''We don't have much time to get Shannon back. Will you help us?'' Abby asked.

''Tell me what you would require.''

''We're hoping you can provide us with a way to get Wu alone—so Steve can question him. We need to know what he sold the rebels. If we can't get the merchandise Oliver was supposed to deliver, maybe we can make some substitution that they'll find acceptable.'' From the corner of her eye, she saw Steve glance at her in surprise. They hadn't discussed that alternative before, but it had suddenly come to her as a possibility.

''You're asking me to take a big risk,'' the woman said. ''I've made my reputation in this city by providing discreet, safe entertainment for wealthy men. If I lose that reputation, I have nothing.''

''I understand. But the risk to you isn't as great as it might seem, because Wu will not tell anyone what happened." Abby saw the woman was listening to her with sharp attention. Hoping she sounded convincing, she went on to amplify the arguments she'd given to Steve at breakfast the morning before.

"I see you've thought this through very carefully."

"We had to."

"And you'd like one of my girls to entice your quarry upstairs and get him to drop his—guard."

Abby shook her head and slid Steve a sidelong glance. She'd used one argument with him, but she'd have to use a different one with Madame Pearl—one that she wished he didn't have to hear. "No. The girl would have to know what was going on, which could put her in danger. I'll do it."

Steve muttered a curse under his breath.

Abby focused on Madame Pearl's dark eyes.

The woman returned her steady gaze. "You'd take that kind of chance?"

"To save my daughter, I'd take any kind of chance." She glanced quickly at Steve. He'd been about to say something. Instead, he pressed his lips together.

"Well, it won't work unless you can masquerade as one of my young ladies." Madame Pearl looked appraisingly at Abby. "Stand up. Turn around slowly," she demanded brusquely.

Abby swallowed hard and stood.

Madame Pearl studied her critically, taking in her hair, her face, her figure. "I believe that with the right makeup and clothing you could meet my standards. But that's not the difficult part. You'd have to act the role of a prostitute. A woman who is sexually available—for money."

Abby stiffened.

"I told you it wouldn't work," Steve grated.

Abby looked from him to Madame Pearl. "I'll do what I have to do to save Shannon," she repeated. "Besides, Wu's not going to touch me in the public rooms. This establishment is too refined for that."

Madame Pearl nodded, and Abby turned back to Steve. "And you're going to come in very soon after Wu closes the bedroom door behind us."

"That's the plan," he shot back. "But there are no guarantees the timing will be perfect—and Pearl hasn't agreed. She's still considering our request."

As Steve looked at the older woman, Abby saw his inner conflict written on his face. He was half hoping Madame Pearl would tell them the scheme was out of the question. Except, where would that leave them?

The madame folded her hands in her lap, and Abby held her breath.

"You know, from time to time, I've been offered money to set up one of my customers like this," the woman began. "I've always flatly refused, because my reputation is too valuable."

Abby clenched her hands against her middle as if she could hold herself together that way.

She saw Madame Pearl focus on her bloodless knuckles and found that she was powerless to move.

"But the rescue of your child is another matter," the older woman continued. "If the two of you are willing to take the risk, I won't turn you down. But I won't shoulder the responsibility if anything goes wrong." She gave Abby a firm look. "Once you walk through the bedroom door with Wu, you're on your own."

ABBY'S FINGERS tightened around what looked like a glass of white wine. It was mostly water. She was dressed in a leather miniskirt that barely covered her thighs. Her frothy silk blouse dipped low into her cleavage. And her three-inch spike heels were the highest that she could manage without the risk of falling on her face, which she was afraid she might do anyway. Figuratively, if not literally.

Her stomach was in knots. Had been in knots for hours. Her eyes flicked across the room toward Steve. She knew he was aware of her, but he didn't acknowledge her presence. Instead he was pretending to be interested in one of the other seductively clad young women arranged around the room like exotic flowers in a well-tended garden. But Abby was sure he was keeping tabs on her exact location.

The bordello didn't open until early evening. At first only a few businessmen came in to sit at the tables with the girls or stand at the ornate marble bar that dominated one side of the parlor. More than one looked at Abby and leaned closer to Madame Pearl to ask a question. But the proprietor told them that the new girl wasn't available.

As the latest man's face registered disappointment, Abby shifted uncomfortably in her seat. How long was she going to have to sit here? she wondered. She tried to remember all the pointers Madame Pearl had given her and all the things she'd said about her customers. Some of the men here tonight only wanted to drink and talk to a beautiful woman. But the majority had come for more explicit sexual entertainment.

There was a lull in the conversation around Abby, and she looked up to see a solid, broad-shouldered man standing in the doorway. His face was instantly recognizable from the photographs she'd seen. It was Tang Wu.

He was shorter than Abby had imagined, and his face was more lined that she'd expected.

Wu and Madame Pearl were speaking quietly near the door. Abby saw the arms dealer glance eagerly in her direction and met his appraising gaze without flinching. When a smile played at the corners of his thin lips, she answered in kind.

Show time.

As the madame led Wu across the room, Abby clenched her hands in her lap, feeling her nails dig into her palms. From the corner of her eye she saw that Steve's attention was focused on the three of them. *Oh, God,* she thought, *don't let him give the game away.*

However, Wu wasn't paying any attention to Steve, or to the other people in the room watching the little scene with interest. "My dear, you're quite delectable. And talented, my good friend Madame Pearl tells me."

"I hope she hasn't been exaggerating my abilities," Abby said with the air of a woman who knew she was good at what she did.

"She didn't exaggerate your charm," he said smoothly.

His English was almost flawless.

"Can I refill your drink?" he asked, as if they were meeting at a social instead of a business occasion.

"Yes, please."

When he picked up her glass and turned toward the bar, Madame Pearl gave her a quick look. Although it was probably meant to be encouraging, it made Abby's blood congeal. "He's quite taken with you," she whispered.

Abby fixed on the confident set of Wu's shoulders as he moved toward the bar. He was a man who knew he was in charge of this situation. Well, she'd have to turn the tables on him.

A few moments later Wu was back at her side holding two flutes of champagne.

"I'd like to get to know you before we go upstairs," he confided.

Abby's heart was thumping so hard inside her chest that she marveled it didn't make the outside of her blouse flutter in rhythm. She hoped that wasn't what Wu was staring at. More likely, he was just enjoying her cleavage. If he only knew why her breasts were so large and rounded, she thought, he'd fall off his chair.

"You find my interest amusing?" he asked, and she realized she would have to guard her expression more carefully.

"Amusing? No, I was thinking about how much we're going to enjoy each other in a little while."

"Just so." He took a long pull of his champagne and sat back, studying her the way a new trainer might study a prize racehorse. "I always wonder why a woman gravitates toward this profession."

Abby licked her lips provocatively, hoping she could cut the conversation short. "Well, there's a certain satisfaction in getting paid for something you'd seek out anyway."

"Ah, yes."

"Talking is never the best way to get to know another person," Abby murmured. "There are much more intimate, more gratifying ways."

She saw excitement flare in Wu's dark eyes and felt a kind of excitement erupt inside herself. It was the same thrill a deep sea fisherman experiences as he plays a giant marlin.

Then Wu reached out to cover her hand with his, and she needed every ounce of willpower not to flinch.

"You're right. Let's go upstairs and enjoy ourselves."

Abby rose. Her heart leapt into her windpipe as Wu's hand pressed into the small of her back. It was a hard, muscular hand. A hand that could inflict a great deal of pain—and would, if he realized what she was planning. Still, she didn't cringe as she allowed herself to be escorted from the room. Behind her, she could feel Steve's eyes boring into the back of her head.

She sensed tension and anticipation in the man behind her as they stepped into the hall. Still, she was the one leading the way toward the stairs. Did that mean he was going to let her take charge of the evening? She'd have to persuade him that was what he really wanted.

All the bedrooms on the hall had names. The Satin Room. The Orchid Room. The Room of Dreams. Abby paused before the door of the Red Room, her hand frozen on the knob.

She'd come up here to look inside several hours ago. So she knew what she'd find. All the unpleasant equipment a man such as Wu enjoyed. Downstairs she'd convinced herself she was only a player in a game. Once she stepped across this threshold, she would be at Tang Wu's mercy—in a very dangerous setting.

She glanced surreptitiously back down the hall, hoping against hope to see Steve on the stairs—and knowing that it was much too early. It might seem like a century, but probably less than a minute had elapsed since she and Wu had gotten up.

He was right behind her. So close, she could feel his breath on her neck. She hadn't known until this moment how vulnerable she was going to feel. Alone with a man who could do anything he wanted to her.

Abby steeled herself for the sound of the door closing behind them. It was very soft, like a sinister caress.

Chapter Ten

For a moment Abby felt only her own icy fear. Then Wu's hands were on her, stroking her arms, and his mouth touched down on her nape.

"I knew which woman Madame Pearl had selected for me as soon as I walked into the parlor. I love your pale skin and your green eyes. You're going to please me very well," he murmured.

All her careful plans floated away like mist in her head. Then the feel of his fingers inching up under her breasts released her, and she was in control again. She slipped out of his grasp, her movements as slow as she could make them. Turning, she reached to take a riding crop from the rack along the wall. With a light stroke, she ran the tip down the front of his shirt, stopped to circle his belt buckle and then slide lower.

"Yes. And I'm going to tease you until you beg me for mercy."

Abby knew immediately from his sharply indrawn breath that he liked her suggestion—and the moves she was making.

The knowledge gave her courage. "Take off your shirt," she ordered in a voice that suddenly held the authority of an army drill instructor. "Just your shirt."

While he complied, Abby looked around the room, her eyes flicking from the elaborate brass headboard to a set of handcuffs hanging on the wall.

Wu was breathing hard. "And your blouse. Take it off. I like to see a woman's breasts when she works on me," he choked out.

"Not yet. We're going to do this my way, remember? Lie down. And raise your hands up toward the headboard."

For a moment Abby was afraid he wasn't going to follow directions. Then he stretched out on the satin spread, raising his arms as she'd directed.

Abby cuffed one wrist, threaded the chain around a brass rail, and secured the other wrist. She breathed a sigh of relief as she heard the lock snap home.

Stepping away, she gazed at the man on the bed, who still didn't know he'd been suckered. She'd done it. Thank the Lord, she'd done it.

As she looked around the chamber wondering what to do next, a door in the wall opened and Steve came through, his face a grim mask as he advanced toward the bed.

Wu stared at him. Fear flickered in his eyes, but only for a second. "Ah, you do have a surprise for me," he murmured, looking from Steve to Abby. "Madame Pearl said you were inventive."

"Yeah, very inventive," Steve grated, still advancing.

Wu tried to draw away from the intruder's acid voice and harsh features. Before Steve reached him, something heavy crashed against the wall on the other side of the room.

Abby whirled just in time to see a second hidden door burst inward. Then a tall, solidly built man careered into the room, shouting urgently in Chinese.

Abby couldn't understand the words, but she recognized the warning tone.

A bodyguard? But Madame Pearl had said—

Wu's expression changed from fear to anger. Pulling at the cuffs, he tried and failed to free his hands. However, his legs were entirely free, and he was still wearing his shoes. Drawing up his knees, he gave a powerful kick, his feet colliding squarely with the wall of Steve's stomach.

Abby heard the air *whoosh* out of her husband's chest as he doubled over in pain. In the next second, the bigger man was on him, landing a blow to his jaw that sounded as if it had broken teeth. A second followed.

Acting purely on instinct, Abby snatched a larger whip from the wall and brought it down with all her strength against the bodyguard's neck. He cried out at the totally unexpected pain, twisting toward the source of the attack.

Abby still couldn't understand what he was saying, but she knew he was cursing at her as he lunged forward. Raising her arm, she snapped the leather coil down again in another stinging swipe, this time catching the side of his face and leaving a six-inch red welt.

From the corner of her eye, she saw Wu twisting wildly on the bed, struggling to free his hands, but thankfully the cuffs held.

With a groan, Steve pushed himself to his feet and stood, swaying and trying to catch his breath. As he saw the big man charge toward his wife, he gathered himself and sprang forward. He reached the assailant just before his fingers connected with Abby's neck.

Pulling the intruder back, Steve hooked his hand under his chin and slammed him against the wall. The collision would have put a lesser opponent out of commission. This man was apparently made of tempered steel. Staggering up, he rounded on Steve, with the desperation of a fighter who knows he has to win in the next few moments.

Knowing Steve was already hurt, Abby cast her gaze frantically around the room. A heavy metal chain hung at the end of the wall. Yanking it free, she swung it over her head, and flung it toward the guard's skull.

It hit with a sickening crack, and he went down like a sack of rocks tossed off the side of a bridge.

Steve collapsed, panting loudly. Abby scurried to the wall rack. Snatching down another pair of handcuffs, she secured the intruder to an iron ring at the bottom of the wall. Then, with a rope and some skills she hadn't utilized since Girl Scout camp, she hog-tied his legs. It wasn't an elegant job, but it would hold him.

The whole time, Wu was bellowing at her from the bed. Abby tuned him out as she tugged on the bodyguard's bonds to test their stoutness. Satisfied that he wasn't going to get loose and slaughter them both, she rushed to Steve. He'd propped himself into a sitting position and was leaning back against the wall, staring at her. Following the direction of his gaze, she discovered that in the fracas, the front of her blouse had ripped and she was in danger of giving Mr. Wu the kind of view he'd requested. Quickly she pulled the shirt-tails from her waistband and tied them securely under her breasts. Then she sank to the floor beside Steve.

"Are you all right?" she questioned softly.

"More or less." He worked his jaw experimentally. "I came in here to save you from a fate worse than death, but I think you kept that guy from pounding me into dog meat."

Abby pressed close to him, and his arms circled her back. His head drooped to her shoulder.

"I was frightened," she whispered.

His grip on her body tightened. "So was I. For you. But I think you can take care of yourself better than I realized."

"I just grabbed the first thing that came to hand. It turned out to be a whip."

"I guess we're damn lucky Wu doesn't have a feather pillow fetish."

Abby's lips quirked. "Yeah." Just then, a flash of movement caught the corner of her eye, and she swung around, her body braced for another attack. But it was only Madame Pearl, standing on the other side of the ruined door, where Wu couldn't see her. She beckoned urgently.

Pushing herself up, Abby made a wide circle around the bed. The moment she gained the adjoining room, she turned accusingly to the older woman. "You said Wu didn't bring a bodyguard when he came here."

Madame Pearl craned her neck toward the man on the floor. "Another one of my customers vouched for him—Hung Lee, he calls himself—so I didn't know he had anything to do with Mr. Wu. Now I realize he's always been here at the same time Wu visits." She sighed. "There's never been any trouble before, so I wasn't aware he was on guard duty."

Madame Pearl peered at Steve, who had gotten up and gone to inspect the intruder's bonds. "When your husband followed Wu out of the room, Lee followed *him,* only I didn't realize what was happening because I was talking to one of my other customers. He wasn't accompanied by any of my girls, so I came up here." The madame gave Abby a long look. "You know, I'm wondering why I agreed to this crazy scheme of yours. I have half a mind to call this whole thing off."

"It's too late for that. The damage is already done."

"I know." She gestured toward Lee. "Move him over here so my guards can take him away before he wakes. And then get about your business. I want you out of my house as soon as possible."

"Thank you for your tolerance," Abby forced out. Then she hurried back into the Red Room to confer with Steve.

As Steve closed the hidden door through which Lee had entered, the arms dealer raised his head slightly.

Abby marveled at his composure. He looked remarkably calm for a man who was shackled to a brass headboard and facing two dangerous assailants.

"We've met, haven't we?" he said to Steve.

"Several years ago. I'll save you the trouble of showing my picture around town. I'm Steve Claiborne," he replied, as if they were getting acquainted again at a private box at the races. "I used to run an air freight business with Oliver Gibbs."

Wu gave no sign that the names meant anything to him, but the calculating look on his face told Abby that he was sizing up her husband. His next words were amazingly pragmatic. "I'm not going to plead for mercy. Tell me what you want, and I will supply it. If it's money, you're in luck. I have a great deal of it, as you doubtless know."

Steve seemed in no hurry to accept the conversational gambit. Drawing up a chair near the headboard, he sat down, stretched out his legs, and crossed them at the ankles.

Quietly Abby stepped out of Wu's line of sight. The man had already lost enough face in this transaction. Interrogation by a woman would only add insult to injury.

Steve gave her a half nod as if he'd already come to the same conclusion. Then he turned his full attention back to the man on the bed. "You can keep your money. All we want is information."

"What if I can't supply it?"

"Oh, I think you can." He let the observation hang in the air for several moments. "We want to know what Amarjit Singh bought from you."

Wu pushed himself up on the bed, so that his arms were at a slightly more comfortable angle. "Are you working for Singh? Or are you with the CIA?"

"Neither. And since you're not going to acknowledge the connection on your own, I'd better mention we know Oliver Gibbs was supposed to deliver your cargo to Singh."

"Then why don't you ask Gibbs the details? Or has he already told you what's going on? Are you here to negotiate for him? If you are, maybe you don't know the whole story. Get him to explain why he disappeared with the cargo," Wu shot back. "Or can't you find him, either?"

Steve turned and exchanged a quick glance with Abby. Now they knew for sure that Wu hadn't taken the cargo back. At least, if he wasn't lying.

"Oh, we found him, all right. But we're not going to be talking to him unless it's at a séance, which isn't a very reliable form of communication, I'm afraid."

"He's dead?"

From the sidelines, Abby studied the expression on Wu's face. For just a moment, she saw a flicker of alarm. Then it vanished.

Was he afraid of what she and Steve might do to him? Maybe. But that wasn't why he'd just cringed.

The two men were still talking. Abby came forward and touched Steve's arm. When he turned to look at her questioningly, she drew him away.

"I got a surprise ready for Wu this afternoon." Quickly she explained her plan and picked up the small metal box she'd prepared after her session in the beauty parlor. Inside was a glass vial of peroxide. It was co-cooned in several plastic bags.

"I've brought what you asked for from the safe," she said to Steve, pitching her voice so Wu could hear her.

"Good."

Taking the closed container, he turned back to the arms dealer, who was watching them impassively. "As we told you, we don't know what Oliver Gibbs was supposed to be transporting to the ILA," Steve said. "But we did take the liberty of bringing some of the substance with us." As he spoke, he held up the little metal chest.

Wu's gaze focused on the box, and Abby saw his skin pale.

"Whatever's in here killed Oliver, didn't it?" Steve asked.

Wu shrugged. "I don't know what killed him."

"I think you do." Steve thrust the closed container toward the man on the bed. "What is it?"

"You're bluffing. There's nothing in there," Wu tossed back. "You wouldn't take a chance like that." He was obviously making a tremendous effort to maintain his composure.

"Maybe I was too stupid to know better. So why don't you tell me what's in Pandora's box." Steve opened the chest and took out the small, plastic-wrapped vial.

Wu's eyes grew round and his body stiffened as Steve began to unseal the outer bag. When he took out the glass vial, the pungent odor of peroxide filled the room.

The arms dealer uttered an exclamation in Chinese that Abby couldn't understand. But there was no mistaking the edge of horror in his voice as he tried to scramble toward the other side of the bed. The handcuffs kept him from moving very far.

As Steve began to pull at the stopper, the biting smell of peroxide grew stronger. Even though she knew what it was, Abby recoiled. But her reaction was nothing compared to Wu's. A fine sheen of perspiration broke out on his forehead and chest.

"If you don't talk, I'm going to pour it right over your heart," Steve said in a steely voice.

Wu finally broke. With a scream, he lunged as far away as the cuffs would allow. "No!" he shrieked. "Close it up. Get it away from me. Get it out of here."

Steve's fingers paused. "What is it?"

"Poison! It's poison," their captive gasped. "Get it out of here."

"Poison? What kind of poison?"

"Get it out of here," Wu repeated, "before it's too late. For all of us."

"What kind of poison?" Steve persisted.

"Russian. From a chemical weapons plant. Wrap it back up. Get it out of the house, I beg you."

Steve pressed the stopper firmly back into the little vial. Then he slipped the plastic bags into place once more. Wu's eyes never left him as he put the vial back in the box.

Abby stepped forward. "Does it have a name?"

"Nothing you'd recognize."

"Try us."

"Omega."

Omega. The final letter of the Greek alphabet. A word that had come to symbolize the end.

Involuntarily, Abby shuddered and looked at Steve. He pulled her toward the corner of the room and handed her the box. "Never heard of it. But it's a good bet the CIA has."

"Get it out of here," Wu pleaded from the bed once more. "It's dangerous to be in the same room with it."

"Or the same plane. Like Oliver," Abby bit out, her hands tightening on the little chest.

"It was supposed to be properly packaged," Wu insisted. "I don't know what went wrong."

"And if it wasn't wrapped up nice and tight, would it now be contaminating the whole area around where it's stored? Would the plants and animals be dead?" Abby asked, her voice low and grating.

Wu swallowed convulsively and began to babble in Chinese.

Steve grabbed him by the shoulders and shook him. "Don't fall apart yet. You're going to tell us everything you know about Omega, or we're going to smear the stuff on your skin like suntan lotion."

For a moment, the arms dealer's eyes turned upward, and Abby was afraid he was going to faint. Then he managed to get a grip on himself. His eyes focused on Steve and flicked to the box in Abby's hand. "If you've handled it, you've sealed your death warrant."

Chapter Eleven

"We thought we took proper precautions," Steve bit out. "If we've miscalculated, we might as well take you with us."

Wu flattened himself against the headboard and began to speak rapidly. "No, please. Maybe I'm mistaken—"

"I want the truth, damn it! How fast does it kill? What's the mechanism?"

"My Russian contact said significant exposure is fatal within twenty-four hours."

Steve looked back at Abby, and she nodded. They'd passed that milestone.

"It disrupts the central nervous system. There were also birth defects in research animals, and chromosome damage at relatively low levels of exposure."

The words sank into Abby's brain like shards of razor-sharp ice. She felt the chill seep into every cell of her body and then pepper her skin with goose bumps. *Chromosome damage.* At relatively low levels of contact.

Omega hadn't killed them. But could they ever have another child?

Steve swung to look at her. Their eyes locked, and she saw raw pain that mirrored what she felt inside.

But he said nothing, *could* say nothing in front of Tang Wu. Instead, he settled into the chair again and leaned close to the man on the bed.

"I think it's time to stop playing games," he said, his raspy voice sending a chill up her spine.

Knowing she had to follow his lead, she set down the box and crossed back to the bed. She and Steve had to find out as much as they could. Later she could scream and beat her fists against the wall in anguish.

"So we've established Omega is highly toxic," Steve pressed. "What's the delivery system?"

"Variable. It could be put into a city's reservoir, or an airport's air-conditioning system. It's designed to use against large populations."

Abby's fingers dug into her husband's shoulder. If they turned over Omega to Singh, millions of people could die. If they didn't cooperate, he'd kill their baby.

"Why did Oliver take it?" Steve demanded.

Wu shrugged.

"I think you know. And we're going to make you tell us," Abby grated. It was hard not to wish that the bottle she'd brought from the beauty shop really did contain Omega. She could picture herself pouring it all over the man on the bed. Except that would reduce her to his level.

Apparently he had no trouble keying in to her anger. His head twisted toward the closet where she'd set the box, and a fresh crop of perspiration sprouted on his forehead.

"Mr. Gibbs tried to hold me up for more money. I declined, and he disappeared."

"With Oliver dead, there's no way to know if that's true."

Wu's eyes met Steve's. "But there's no reason we both shouldn't profit from the, uh, present situation.

Fortuitously, you know where Gibbs stashed the shipment. You've proved your resourcefulness. Make sure the merchandise is packaged properly and complete the delivery for me, and I'll double the offer I made Gibbs.''

"You know where Singh is?'' Steve asked in a steady voice.

"In a desert encampment west of New Delhi.''

Abby saw the sudden tension in Steve's shoulders. She kept her gaze studiously away from his.

"Singh moves his headquarters frequently. But I've been keeping tabs on him. If you tell me where to send the coordinates, I'll be back to you in just a few hours.''

Abby fought to contain the hope swelling in her breast.

Steve looked as if he were weighing the pros and cons of a tempting business offer. "All right,'' he said. "I can't do anything more for Oliver. I'll play ball with you. On certain conditions.''

"What?''

"Don't assume I'm crazy enough to trust you. Give me a contact number, and *I'll* get back to you at my convenience.''

Wu reluctantly complied.

"Test it,'' Steve told Abby.

Using the phone on a table across the room, she confirmed that they had Wu's private business line.

"All right, so you're playing that part straight,'' Steve said. "But don't try to locate us. And don't even think about retaliating against Madame Pearl. She didn't know what we'd intended to do.''

"You expect me to believe that?'' Wu shot back.

"It doesn't matter whether you do or not. If anything suspicious happens to her, I'll make sure everyone who matters to you hears the story of how you were trussed up like a steer carcass at an old-fashioned Texas barbecue. Do you understand?''

''Yes,'' Wu managed through clenched teeth.

Abby wasn't going to take his word on it. Stepping forward, she reached for the arms dealer's hand. When her flesh touched his, she fought the bile rising in her throat. But she didn't release him.

As she began to slip the diamond and ruby ring off his finger, he clenched his fist. ''No.''

Steve saw what she was doing and pried his hand open again. With his help, she removed the ring she suspected Wu hadn't taken off since he'd received it.

''What are you doing?'' he gasped.

''Call it an insurance policy,'' Abby replied as her own fist closed around the warm metal. ''I know you got this from your grandfather. I know you consider it your source of good fortune. You'll get it back when we've delivered the merchandise and gotten out of Singh's camp.''

''No. Wait,'' Wu cried as she backed way. ''Come back with that.''

Ignoring him, she turned and left the room, stopping on the way out to scoop up the box of quackery she'd left in the closet.

WE CAN FIND out where Shannon is. We can rescue her.

Abby repeated those words over and over in her head on the way back to the hotel.

Yet at the same time she felt a terrible hollow void inside her chest, like a massive gunshot wound.

In the space of a few heartbeats, Wu had told them the facts about Omega. And the stakes had changed so completely that she could barely draw a solid breath into her lungs.

Her hands squeezed into helpless fists. She loved Shannon. God, how she loved her. She'd do anything to get her daughter back, including give up her own life. But deep in the cavern of her mind, she'd buried a secret treasure in a tightly padlocked box. Shannon could never be replaced. Yet if the worst happened and there was no way she could save this baby, she could love another one just as much.

Only now there was never going to be another baby. Wu had told them Omega caused chromosome damage at low levels of exposure. She and Steve had been exposed outside the temple. And there was no way they could risk having another child.

On robotic legs, she walked toward the elevator. She was aware of Steve beside her. He'd kept his arm curled protectively around her since they'd left Madame Pearl's. But she dared not lean against him, dared not let go of her tight control. If she did, she'd start to sob.

Steve led her down the hall. Then he leaned down to unlock the door. It closed behind them and they were finally alone.

Blindly she reached for him. "Wu said...we can't...any more babies..." she choked out and couldn't finish the rest of the sentence.

He folded her into his embrace. She clung to him, the fear and sorrow coming out of her in a great rush. She wept softly. He murmured low, soothing words as his hands stroked her hair, her shoulders.

"Abby, sweetheart. Don't think about the bad stuff now. Think about what else he told us. It's going to be all right. We're going to get Shannon back. Wu will give us the location of the camp, and Jason can confirm the information." There was a deep, rock-solid certainty in his voice that helped calm her.

With a shuddering little sigh, she let him lead her to the sofa.

He nestled her in his arms. "And we don't know for sure about Omega, or how much exposure we got. There are tests. Your friend Katie Martin can tell us what to do. Genetics is her field."

It was a spark of hope, and she clung to it as she clung to him. But when she raised her tear-streaked face toward his, she saw the stark landscape of his countenance. She knew this man so well, knew he'd been trying to hold himself together, too. He was doing his damnedest to be optimistic and strong for her, yet he was deeply troubled.

"Don't try to keep it all inside," she murmured.

He brushed a kiss across her forehead.

"Tell me what you're thinking. Maybe whatever's in your mind isn't as bad as you imagine."

Still, he hesitated before starting to speak in a harsh whisper. "I'm the guy who didn't want kids in the first place. So why do I feel as if I'm standing on the edge of a cliff and the ground is crumbling away under my feet?"

"Because you love Shannon. You don't want to lose her. And at the same time, you're feeling guilty because in the back of your mind there was always the knowledge that if the worst happened, we could make another baby."

"That's not the way a father's supposed to feel about his child, is it?" he grated.

The pain in his eyes made her heart turn over. Gently, she took his face between her hands. "Oh, Steve. Don't. How do you think I knew all that?"

"You're a psychologist."

"Not now. Now I'm a frightened mother." She swallowed convulsively. "I love Shannon so much. But deep in my heart I told myself I could love another baby just as truly. Just the way you could. When we made love that morning in the hotel, we didn't do anything about birth control. Maybe I was even hoping I'd get pregnant. Does that mean I love Shannon any less?" she whispered.

"Of course not. *Of course not.* Don't ever think such a thing."

"Then believe me when I tell you your reactions are just as normal."

"I thought I must be like my father. I thought—"

Her hand moved to his lips, silencing him. "No! I never met the man, but I have a pretty good idea of what he was like."

"How could you?"

"From the things you've told me about your childhood. I know your father was strong-willed, like you. He was afraid to rely on anyone but himself. But he didn't have a clue about what was important in life. You do. He didn't know how to care about anyone but himself. You do."

"That's the way you see me?"

"Yes. Strong and aggressive. Also protective and compassionate, but it makes you nervous when you have to show me anything but the strength."

A half smile flickered around his lips. "I had a pretty hard shell around me when I met you. I'd still have it if you hadn't crashed your way through."

"For a little while, I forgot how to do it," she said in a low voice. "Right after Shannon was born, my head was pretty messed up." She looked away for a moment. "My emotions were out of control. Maybe I was having something like a postpartum depression. I don't know. But I was afraid to lean on your strength, to ask you to help me. And that was a big mistake."

"Abby."

"I get as much from you as you do from me. I was ready to fall apart when we left Madame Pearl's. But you pulled me back to coherence. I couldn't have gotten through this without you."

He folded her close. She felt his Adam's apple bob. "Sweetheart, I didn't like using you to get to Wu."

"I know."

"But we've finally made a big breakthrough. We *can* rescue Shannon. That's the most important thing to remember now."

"Mmm-hmm." She tried to block out everything else. Yet it was still impossible to simply forget the new fear, the new uncertainty. Until she held Shannon in her arms again, until she had her child safely back in Baltimore, terror would be just below the surface of every thought, waiting to grab her.

She felt Steve's shoulders heave and knew that no matter what he tried to tell her, he was just as tormented as she.

Instinctively she raised her head, seeking his mouth with hers, needing him more now than she had ever needed anyone in her life. He was the only one who could take away the terrible pain. The only one who could make her believe that everything really would come out all right.

And she had to do the same for him, too. Because she loved him so much.

"Sweetheart. Sweetheart," he murmured, his lips brushing back and forth against hers. Slowly, as if neither of them had any choice, the kiss deepened, lengthened, changed from comforting to carnal.

At the same time, there was no stopping their hands as they began to move over each other's bodies, giving and taking the most basic kind of solace.

Tenderly his fingers stroked over her breasts, and she whimpered.

"Am I hurting you? Are they still sore?"

"A little. But it feels so good."

"Lord, yes." He kissed her again. Deeply, greedily. And she could taste the desire on his lips. "Ahh, Abby, let me love you, sweetheart."

Her eyes flew open. "We can't..."

He leaned closer to kiss her cheek. "You'll have to trust me not to get you into trouble."

"I do trust you."

He grabbed her hand, pulling her gently off the couch, guiding her toward the bedroom. He seemed so sure of himself, so she let him take the lead.

Quickly he stripped off all his clothing except his briefs. Then his fingers went to the the ties of her blouse and the pace slowed. She closed her eyes, desperate to lose herself in the achingly sweet pleasure of being with him like this. He knew her so well. He was taking her away from all the pain and sorrow and uncertainty of the past few days—the past few weeks—to a haven in another universe where only the two of them existed.

She knew that making love without being inside her wasn't what he would have chosen. But it wasn't second best, either. They knew each other's bodies, knew how to please and tantalize.

Hands caressed, mouths sought. Strong emotions surged like giant tides of feeling over and around and through them both. Shudders of pleasure racked her slender frame, pleasure rooted in her deep and passionate response to this man. In her deep commitment.

She was aware of nothing but him. Of the two of them, making a safe, secure world of their own. Even if it was only for a little while.

"Oh, Steve, I love you so much. I love you," she sobbed out.

"Abby. Abby." He was trembling, too. His lips were feverish as they moved over her face, her brows, and then back to her mouth for long, fierce, claiming kisses.

Finally, almost without warning, she was past the point of no return, and he was holding her tenderly as a storm of fulfillment swept over her body.

Then it was her turn to give that deep, abiding pleasure back to him.

Chapter Twelve

Abby let out a long sigh of relief as the plane taxied down the runway. Wu had come through with the location of the rebel camp, and Jason had confirmed the coordinates through independent intelligence sources. Now, after hours of frantic preparation, she and Steve were finally on their way back to India.

As she'd anticipated, Steve had tried to persuade her to return to Baltimore and wait for him there. She'd convinced him he needed her to take care of Shannon while he concentrated on getting them in and out of the rebel camp.

As she pretended to catnap in the copilot's seat, she watched Steve from under lowered lashes, marveling at how calm, confident, and efficient he looked as he flew them toward their refueling stop.

"You're not really sleeping, are you?" he asked.

Abby opened her eyes. "No. I was wishing we knew exactly where in the camp Shannon is being kept."

"Somewhere in the women's quarters."

She nodded. She wanted to ask him if he really thought they could pull this off, but she wouldn't. When she'd awakened in the morning, he'd already been on the phone for several hours preparing to take off, ordering supplies, and making arrangements with

Jason for backup help. As soon as they had Shannon, armed helicopters would swoop in and pick them up.

The change in him was dramatic. He'd been hitting his head against brick wall after brick wall since Shannon had been kidnapped. Finally he was in charge of the situation, and he looked as though he was ready to go into hand-to-hand combat with Amarjit Singh. She was praying it didn't come to that.

At the New Delhi airport, they had a meal delivered while the plane was being serviced for the last leg of their flight. Abby pushed some of the food around her plate, but when she saw Steve watching her, she did manage to swallow a few bites. She also tried, unsuccessfully, to relax. They were so close now. She kept picturing herself holding Shannon in her arms again, hugging her, kissing her. She'd been doing it a lot. And she knew it was a bad idea to get so involved in the fantasy. But she couldn't stop herself. Sometimes it was like the morning she'd stood outside Raj Sunduram's house. She felt as if she were really seeing Shannon— really watching her sleep. Then the baby would start to cry, and a woman whose face she couldn't see would come in and pick her up. Abby's stomach would knot. The tantalizing image would dissolve like a desert mirage, and Abby would press her fist against her mouth to keep from screaming.

An hour later they were cleared for takeoff from New Delhi. The weather turned hazy as they left the city behind and flew westward toward the desert. Almost from one moment to the next, the ground disappeared from view under a heavy cloud cover, and Abby felt all her muscles tensing.

"I can't see a thing," she blurted.

"Yeah, but if we can't see the rebels, they can't see us, either. We'll start our descent in a few minutes,"

Steve tossed out. Yet she caught an echo of her edgi-
ness in his voice.

"How far to the flats?"

He didn't answer, and she started to repeat the
question. Then she saw his rigid profile. All his attention was riveted on a rapidly approaching amber cloud.
"What's that?"

"Big trouble! I think we're flying right into a sandstorm. Hold on, I'm going to try to get above it."

Abby gripped the armrests as he nosed the plane
upward abruptly. Her ears popped, and she swallowed
convulsively, praying that the maneuver would work.
In the next moments, however, the cockpit was bathed
in eerie brown shadow as the storm swallowed them up.
The plane began to toss from side to side like a virtual-
reality ride at a futuristic amusement park. Only this
was reality. Steve's hands clenched the controls as he
tried desperately to hold the craft steady, but the little
plane felt like a balsa-wood model caught in a hurricane. The engines began to sputter and strain. Abby
listened to the unnatural grit in their hum.

Raw fear tightened every nerve in her body. "Steve,
what's wrong with the engines?"

Beside her, his tan face had drained sheet-white.
"Sand in the generator!" All around them alarms were
going off. Fine grains of sand hit the windshield like a
constant spray of bullets.

"Get on the radio and holler *Mayday*," Steve
shouted.

Grabbing the microphone, Abby tried to hang on to
it as the plane made another dive. "CL-6, Mayday,
Mayday. Plane in trouble."

The only response was a loud crackle of static.
Frantically she tried again. "Mayday, Mayday."
Again, there was no answer.

Despite Steve's efforts, the air speed indicator was falling rapidly, and the vacuum gyro—their guide to the horizon—was spinning wildly, like a weather vane in a thunderstorm.

Beside her, he uttered a pungent expletive. "Put your hands over your face. We're going down."

ABBY FELT as if she'd ridden a tornado from Kansas to the Land of Oz. Surprised that she could still move, she opened her eyes. When she did, she found Steve bending over her, trying to unsnap her shoulder belt. Blood ran down his face from a dozen cuts.

"You're hurt," she gasped.

"Nothing serious. How are you?"

She flexed her shoulders and winced.

"Anything broken?" Steve's hands traveled gently over her body.

"No. I'm just shaken up, I think." Still a bit dazed, she looked around. The instrument panel was scrunched up like an accordion. Through the shattered windshield, she could see that the plane was tilted sideways, the nose and one wing wedged in a sand dune. But at least they'd passed through the worst of the storm. Only a light wind blew a fine powder of sand through the jagged edges of glass. "Did we land or crash?"

"A little of both, I guess."

"Don't . . . don't we have to get out of here?"

"There's one good thing about landing in sand. It absorbs any leaking fuel."

Assured that the plane wasn't going to catch fire, Abby reached her arms out to Steve, and he pulled her tightly against his chest. For several heartbeats they held each other, rejoicing that they were alive and in amazingly good shape. "Oh, God, Steve, I was so scared."

"I was, too, sweetheart."

"But you saved us. I guess I didn't know how good a pilot you really are!"

"Well, now you'd be better off with an expert on Indian geography."

"You don't know where we are?"

"With luck, within fifty miles or so of our rendezvous place."

"Maybe we should send out another Mayday."

Abby's gaze followed Steve's wry glance to the mangled radio. "Then again, maybe Jason's men heard our first call and are on their way to rescue us."

"Don't count on it, Abby," he said in a flinty voice.

"What aren't you telling me?"

"You remember on *Mission Impossible* how the secretary would always say he'd disavow any knowledge of the operation if things went wrong?"

She nodded and wiped away the sand sticking to her forehead.

"Well, that's what I had to agree to with Jason's backup team. It was risky enough mounting the operation without the CIA finding out. The local talent wasn't willing to stick around if anything got screwed up. I think we're on our own."

Abby was pretty sure he'd added that "I think" as a last-minute palliative for her benefit.

"We can get out of here by ourselves," Steve murmured.

She raised her eyes to his and saw fierce determination—overlaying troubling doubt. He was damn worried. So was she. But whatever happened, she wasn't going to give in to hopelessness.

She squeezed his hand. "We will."

He swallowed. "We've got a lot to do." He picked up one of her hands and inspected the back. "Let's see if we can find something to put on your cuts."

"Yours, too. I packed a first-aid kit in the back, if we can get to it."

Keeping an arm around her shoulders, he helped her maneuver over the slanted floor and debris to the back of the cabin.

By the time they had attended to their injuries and taken stock of the supplies, the sun had dipped to the horizon, and the desert heat had dropped a few notches from broiling to merely sweltering. Steve and Abby climbed out a hole in the side of the plane where the right wing had once been attached, to check the damage. The aircraft lay on its belly, its nose and the other wing wedged at a forty-five degree angle into a steep sand dune. In addition, the tail section had cracked on impact.

"We were lucky as hell," Steve growled. "But at least old CL-6 is still good for shelter. I know it's hard to believe, but the temperature drops off pretty sharply when the sun goes down."

Abby wiped a trickle of sweat from her neck. "Sounds good to me."

"We've got enough water and food for a couple of days, and tomorrow we'll lay out a message in the sand."

"If someone heard my Mayday call, they could already be on their way to rescue us," Abby added hopefully.

"Yeah." Steve's tone was not as optimistic.

THE FULL MOON filtered through the cracks in the fuselage, casting eerie shadows of black on gray around the walls. On a makeshift bed of seat cushions, Steve lay with Abby cradled in his arms, wishing he could sleep. He'd been too damn confident that everything was going to fall into place for him this time. He'd also been a fool to let Abby persuade him that it was safe for her to come. He'd regretted the decision a thousand times since he'd first seen that yellow cloud on the horizon. His arms tightened around her, and he could feel her pulse beating evenly against his hand. At least she was exhausted enough to conk out.

God, he loved her so much. And he'd felt so helpless to make things come out right for her. When Wu had told them about Omega, he'd wanted to leap up and start battering the man with his fists. Instead he'd calmly continued with the interrogation. And he'd thought it had paid off. He'd thought he could finally rescue Shannon. And maybe, just maybe, the three of them could go home and be a normal family.

And now this. His gaze swept around the crumpled plane.

If he'd thought he could walk out of here and find help, he would have done it. But it wasn't going to be so good for Abby if he ended up dead from lack of water. And he didn't even know whether it was safe to leave her in the plane alone.

He cursed silently. No matter how strongly he felt as if he needed to *do something,* there was absolutely nothing he could accomplish until morning. Finally he closed his eyes and tried to breath deeply and evenly. He was so exhausted that it worked. But even as he sank into a fitful doze, he kept wondering what their chances were of saving Shannon and whether he could even get his wife out of this alive.

Hours later, a noise outside brought Steve instantly awake, and his eyes flashed open. Above him, a large male body blocked out most of the moonlight.

"Who are you?"

"We come to rescue you." Behind the speaker, two more men gathered around the hole where the wing had been. They were all dressed in shorts and loose-fitting shirts.

"How did you find us?" Steve asked, maneuvering to get a better look at the trio.

"The radio call."

Abby looked from Steve to the men. "Thank God!" Sitting up, she wiped her hair back from her face.

"You are very lucky, I think," the spokesman responded. "Get up, so we can be on our way."

Despite the congenial words, Steve noted that all three men were holding guns.

"And where are you taking us?"

"To where you were going in the first place, Mr. Claiborne. You are Steve Claiborne, are you not?"

Steve's nerves tightened, but his eyes never wavered from those of the man looking down on him. "Yes."

"Then let us proceed to the Lion's den."

"Fine. That's what we came for."

Steve helped Abby to her feet, feeling her tension under his fingers. She'd been grateful they were being rescued. Then she'd understood the new danger. He kept a steadying hand on her shoulder as their captors hustled them out of the plane.

Abby watched her husband for cues on how to handle the situation. His expression was carefully neutral, but she knew he was working to create an impression—for their captors and her.

Outside, the night air felt cool, and moonlight spilled over barren terrain like liquid silver. But the stark beauty only made her shiver.

Steve helped her struggle up a mountain of sand. It was tough going. Her shoes filled with the fine grains.

And near the crest of the shifting hill, her calf muscles—already stiff and sore—started to cramp.

As she stumbled, Steve's arm tightened around her waist and steadied her before she could fall.

"Hurry!" one of the men urged.

"She's been through a plane crash! She needs to rest," he grated.

"No. The Lion has already been kept waiting too long by you."

"It's all right," Abby murmured. She started moving again, feeling her legs protest with every step she took. Teeth gritted, she made it over the dune and down the other side. Their escort forced them to keep moving. A few hundred yards away, where the sand was hard-packed, stood a waiting helicopter.

The men had given up any pretense of friendliness. Rough hands pushed Abby into a bench seat along one wall. Steve came so fast behind her that she knew he must have been shoved hard.

"Tie them up," the leader ordered gruffly.

Abby threw Steve a panicked glance.

"It'll be okay. They just want us off balance," he whispered, but his jaw was tight and his fists were clenched.

She flinched away from the man with the rope. He pulled her hands forward and secured her wrists and then her ankles with coarse jute. When the binding bit into her flesh, she winced. Steve was also tied up. Sliding over, she pressed her shoulder against his. They sat that way as the helicopter lifted off.

The motion tightened the rope, and she tried to stay as still as possible, fighting her fear as well as the discomfort. They had planned a daring raid on Amarjit Singh. Now his men were bringing them in like confiscated livestock.

A HALF HOUR LATER the chopper landed on the outskirts of Singh's stronghold. One of the men untied Abby, and she tried to shake some feeling into her hands and feet.

When she didn't start to move fast enough to suit him, he prodded her with his gun. "Come. The Lion is waiting."

In the gray dawn, she stumbled toward the camp. Steve was in front of her. One guard led the way and two were behind them. Did they think their prisoners were going to bolt?

They passed several Jeeps parked alongside half a dozen camels. Then came dozens of tents, mostly of the army-surplus variety, scattered over an area the size of a football field. How many men were here? How many women and children? Abby wondered. She suspected that the inhabitants had been told to stay inside for their arrival, because she saw almost no one.

A satellite dish and outdoor latrines were at opposite edges of the enclave.

Abby tried to keep track of their route, but the dwellings were too similar and laid out in too much of a random pattern for her to be sure of where they were going. Finally they came to a halt in front of one of the larger tents.

"*Jathedār*, we have the man and the woman," the leader of the trio announced.

The two subordinates kept Abby and Steve outside for several moments.

Get it over with, Abby wanted to shout. Instead she stood quietly, trying to catch the exchange of information beyond the heavy canvas. But the words were in a language she couldn't understand.

The head man reappeared and ushered them inside onto a muted Indian rug. The interior of the command post was lit with a single oil lamp that cast their shadows as grotesque figures on the slanted canvas walls. A large man with piercing black eyes, a turban and a beard stood in the center of the sparsely furnished area.

"You are Mr. and Mrs. Claiborne, I presume?"

"Yes. And you are the Lion," Steve responded.

"Amarjit Singh," the commander introduced himself. "Why did you try to creep into camp without my knowledge?"

Abby swallowed. Nothing like getting off to a bad start.

"We had no way to contact you," Steve answered.

"I sent a message to your house directing you to Rampur, where you would have received further instructions. You should have stayed home to receive word from me."

Steve acted as if he hadn't heard the dangerous inflection in the other man's voice. "I guess we ought to thank you for rescuing us."

"Despite your best efforts, I have the upper hand."

The cat-and-mouse game made Abby want to scream. "We came for our baby. Do you have her, or don't you?" she demanded.

"The discussion is between me and your husband," Singh told her sharply.

Abby felt her face heat and looked away. Making Singh angry would get her nowhere.

"Yes," Steve agreed. "But if we're going to exchange merchandise, you'll have to show me you have something we want."

The Lion waited several beats. Then he gave another order, and a dark-skinned woman entered carrying a small bundle wrapped in a pink and green receiving blanket. Abby's heart lurched. Shannon. Oh,

God, it was Shannon. Tears welled in her eyes as she ran to the woman's side and snatched up her daughter.

First she hugged her to her breast, feeling an incredible warmth and joy spread through her soul. Then she gently folded back the blanket and ran shaky fingers over her child's tiny body, from her soft hair and little fingers to her curling toes.

"You're just fine," she crooned.

Shannon blinked.

Steve had come up close beside Abby. She glanced at him and swallowed convulsively. He moved his hand to touch the baby, but stopped, his eyes flicking to Singh. The rebel leader was watching them intently, and the satisfied look on his face made the blood in Abby's veins turn to ice.

Ignoring the scrutiny, she tipped her head toward Steve. "Look, she's grown. She's healthy."

Steve's fingers squeezed her arm, but he didn't speak, and Abby knew he was struggling not to give his emotions away.

Singh cleared his throat. "Mrs. Claiborne, you and the baby will leave now so that your husband and I can decide what will happen to you."

Chapter Thirteen

Amarjit Singh took a last swallow from his glass of mint tea. "Now we must well and truly get down to business." He spoke with the precision of a man who'd attended private schools.

Which meant that either he'd been trying to convey a certain impression with the original ransom note or he hadn't personally written it, Steve surmised. "All right," he returned in the same easy tone his host had used. "I'm waiting to hear what you have to say."

Across the tent, he carefully considered the rebel leader. Singh sat cross-legged on one of the plush Oriental rugs that carpeted the tent. His wiry, dark beard hid the bottom part of his face and his bright saffron turban covered his hair. He was dressed in a pair of khaki shorts, a loose-fitting, sleeveless shirt that displayed his muscular arms, and a pair of Nike running shoes. The outfit was accented by a short sword in a scabbard slung diagonally across his chest. Guerilla chic.

After sending Abby and Shannon to the women's compound, he'd left Steve cooling his heels for forty-five minutes. Then he'd invited him into his living quarters. But so far he'd only served tea and sweet cakes, and talked about his hopes of an independent state for the Sikh people and why he'd given up a po-sition of prestige and a comfortable home in the most fertile region of India to live like a camel driver in the desert.

Yet the rebel hospitality and the thought-provoking conversation hadn't lulled Steve into dropping his guard. He knew he was facing a ruthless and unpre-dictable man.

"Let's go back to a previous point we didn't settle," the Lion said. "I carefully worked out a plan to bring you to this camp—without your knowing its exact lo-cation. You didn't pick up the flying instructions to the rendezvous point, yet you were on your way here when your plane went down."

"I didn't get your directions, because I was busy tracking down the arms dealer who was the original supplier of your merchandise. He knew your loca-tion."

"You're lying. Who is this arms dealer?"

Steve kept his gaze steady. "Tang Wu. He has a highly developed information network." He could see the name had registered.

"So you claim. Yet Wu didn't locate Oliver Gibbs. Or did he? Perhaps you should fill me in on exactly what happened to the shipment Gibbs was supposed to deliver."

"I'm not going to fill you in on anything until my wife and daughter are out of this camp."

"You're hardly in a position to make demands."

"Oh, I think I am. Unless I know my family is safe, you won't get your weapons."

"I could have you all killed."

"I'm aware of that. But I'm the only one who knows where Gibbs stashed the shipment. I didn't tell Wu, so you're going to have to deal with me."

"I can deal with you by making you watch your wife and baby staked out in the hot sun."

Steady, Steve told himself. *Steady.* He knew Singh was appraising him, just as he was appraising the rebel. Looking for the weak spots. "Kill them and there will be no way in hell you'll get what you want."

"Maybe I can pry it out of your wife. Do you think she'd like to watch me cut off your...fingers?"

"That would be a waste of your time," Steve answered evenly. "She doesn't have the information you want. I made very sure of that."

"Talk is cheap."

"Perhaps. But consider this bit of intelligence. You're not the only one trying to find out what happened to Oliver Gibbs. The CIA spent a lot of time and effort asking me questions. They didn't get a damn thing, but I've left a sealed envelope to be delivered to them if anything happens to me or my family."

Singh snorted. "The CIA may be keeping tabs on me, but they won't interfere. Just the way they didn't interfere when thousands of my people were killed at the Golden Temple or in their homes."

"I understand your anguish over those murders."

"How could you? You think because you spent a few years piloting cargoes around India that you understand what's going on in this country?"

"If you've had me investigated, you know what happened to my sister. You know how far I was prepared to go to punish the men who killed her. One of them turned out to be very close to me. That didn't stop me from shooting him," Steve said evenly.

Singh held Steve's piercing gaze for several seconds longer. "Meeting an individual is always different from reading about him."

"Yes." Steve's face gave no indication that he was about to play the most risky card in his meager deck. The only way he was going to save Abby and Shannon was to convince Amarjit Singh that Steve Claiborne was as hard and ruthless as the rebel leader. "I understand the use of torture—perhaps not as well as you do, but well enough. How do you think I pried your location out of Tang Wu?"

Singh snorted. "You couldn't get to him unless you were a guest in his home. He's guarded by a small army."

"Except when he goes to a certain bordello to indulge his peculiar sexual tastes. Oh, I got to him, all right, and worked him over pretty thoroughly. That's how I know why the CIA is so interested you."

"You're bluffing!" Singh snapped.

"Bluffing? I don't think so. Make some discreet inquiries. You'll find Wu is out of circulation for a while. I got information out of him he hasn't dared to tell anyone else. I may know more about Omega than you do."

Steve went on, carefully spinning a tale woven of fact and half-truth and speculation about the chemical weapon, knowing that Singh would already have some of the information. But he wouldn't be able to check the rest. He also knew he had the man's undivided attention. "All the information about Omega and your connection to it is in the letter I addressed to the CIA. It will be sent to them if my family and I disappear into the Indian desert."

When he stopped speaking, there was absolute silence inside the tent. Outside, the wind was picking up sand. Was another storm coming? Would that make it impossible to get Abby and Shannon out of here tonight? He wanted them away from the camp as soon as possible, before Singh had a chance for second thoughts.

"Suppose I deal on your terms. What do you want?"

"I want my wife and child back home in Baltimore before I take you to Gibbs's stash."

Singh laughed harshly. "Impossible. I need a closer hold on something you value. I'm willing to send them to New Delhi—with an escort who will make sure that they don't disappear before you fulfill your part of the bargain."

"Your men? According to my information, they've murdered quite a few women and children. What would two more be to them?"

"You don't trust me?" Singh asked.

"No," Steve answered coolly.

"Trust has to begin somewhere. I will send your wife and child with only one man—and the woman who brought me the baby. And when I have the shipment of Omega in my possession, your family will be free to go. As will you."

He could continue the fencing match, but Steve sensed that this was the best he was going to get. "All right. You have a deal."

"YOU LIKE THAT, don't you?" Abby bent and nuzzled her face against the soft skin of Shannon's tummy.

Her daughter was lying on a cotton blanket in the center of a thick rug. For a makeshift changing table, it seemed to be working pretty well.

Shannon kicked her legs and cooed. She must like having that bulky diaper off, Abby thought as she breathed in the delicate scent of Shannon's body, feeling as if her heart would burst with joy.

Oh, God, this was a miracle. Yet even as she clung to her child, she still felt a sharp wedge of fear digging into her soul. The nightmare wasn't over. She and Steve had found Shannon, but they were still at the mercy of Amarjit Singh.

And being separated from Steve now was like having one of her own arms cut off. Where was he? What was Singh doing to him?

Just then, the light inside the tent shifted subtly. Someone was watching. Abby pushed a lock of her hair away from her eyes, turning her head far enough to see a woman standing in the doorway. She held a veil partly across her face, but it didn't hide her nicely shaped brows, her golden skin, or the mixture of curiosity and disdain in her large, dark eyes.

Deliberately Abby finished diapering her daughter. The stranger didn't speak, didn't move, and Abby felt her heart rate accelerate. Had this woman come to take Shannon away?

As if she were confident nothing untoward was going to happen, she turned and looked inquiringly at the visitor.

"I wanted to see if you were comfortable here," the visitor said as she stepped fully into the tent. The hospitable words didn't match the guarded expression in her eyes.

"Yes, thank you for coming to see us."

She let the veil drop away from her face, and Abby was struck by her beauty. "I am the wife of Amarjit Singh. Inder-Jeet," she said in the lilting English so characteristic of her people. "I welcome you to our camp."

"Thank you," Abby replied as she unobtrusively studied the newcomer. Her shining black hair was still modestly covered. Long, baggy trousers hid her figure, and a scarf across her breasts disguised their fullness, but she moved with the self-assurance of a woman secure of her charms.

"I tried to have things ready for you. But we weren't getting the disposable diapers like the ones in the American hospital," she said. "There's only cloth."

"This is fine." Turning, Abby gathered up Shannon and held her tightly.

Inder-Jeet's gaze focused on the blanket-wrapped bundle. Then it roamed over Abby's khaki shorts, camp shirt, and tennis shoes. "We don't meet many women like you."

"Like what?"

"Brave enough to do the same things as the men. But when your plane was going down, it must have been frightening. Were you sorry you'd chosen to make such a dangerous journey?"

"I was afraid, but I wasn't sorry."

"And it was the same when you went to the other man? Oliver Gibbs?"

Abby heard a sudden tension underneath the words. She bent to rub her lips against the silky hair of Shannon's head, hiding her eyes from the other woman's prying gaze. Her thoughts were racing, trying to stay ahead of Inder-Jeet. "Steve and I came here together from Hong Kong," she said, careful that her answer could still be technically considered the truth.

"But your husband was looking for Mr. Gibbs, was he not? Why didn't you go with him?" Inder-Jeet asked.

Abby's breath stilled as she considered the best possible answer. Feeling like a witch of a mother, she tightened her hold on Shannon's thigh, and the baby gave a little squeak of protest.

"Oh, honey. What is it? Is your diaper too tight? Is it pinching your leg?" she asked solicitously, setting her daughter down again on the blanket and starting to fiddle with the safety pin as she scrambled to assess how much this woman already knew. Was this woman trying to find out more than Steve had already told Singh? Or was she here to discover if Steve had lied to the rebel leader . . . ?

Fear for Steve leapt inside her again, and she struggled to tamp it down so she could think.

"You didn't talk to Mr. Gibbs?" Inder-Jeet persisted.

"There was little point in my joining my husband until we knew where to find Shannon."

"But you were so anxious to get your baby back."

"Someone had to stay in Baltimore in case further messages came from Singh. So Steve left me there." She raised her gaze to the other woman, hoping she could project her feeling of frustration and desertion when she'd thought Steve was abandoning her to chase phantoms. "We didn't agree, but he didn't give me any choice about it. Later I took matters into my own hands, and flew to meet him. That convinced him how serious I was about joining the search, I think."

Inder-Jeet pleated the edge of her scarf with her fingers. "So your husband had already located the missing weapons."

Abby murmured her agreement.

"Where did he say the shipment was being stored?"

"He didn't tell me." Convinced she knew what Inder-Jeet had come to find out, Abby spoke the bald-faced lie in the same tone with which she'd offered her half-truths.

"Why not?" Inder-Jeet persisted in her not very skillful interrogation.

"We decided it was safer for me if I didn't know where to find the weapons," Abby answered, feeling a hundred times more confident than she had a few minutes ago. Picking up Shannon again, she held her daughter against her chest and stared at her visitor.

The young woman sighed and moved toward the door of the tent. "Well, I know you must be tired, so I'll leave you to rest."

"Thank you." Torn between getting rid of the intruder and seeing to Shannon's needs, Abby cleared her throat. "Uh, is there a cradle for the baby?"

"The little hammock."

Inder-Jeet retrieved a folded contraption of sticks and fabric lying near one of the tent walls. Earlier Abby had wondered what it was for. Now she watched Singh's wife deftly open the sticks into a cross-braced frame that held the hammock.

Testing the balance, Abby found it was very stable. "I see. Yes. Thank you."

"You can rock her in it," Inder-Jeet said as she backed toward the door of the tent. "And tell the guard at the door if you need anything else."

Alone again, Abby stood in the middle of the tent, feeling light-headed, hoping that she'd really passed the test.

If she could have five minutes alone with Steve. No, five seconds. If she could just look into his eyes, she'd know what their chances were.

Shannon stirred in her arms, and she lowered the baby into the cloth sling. Straightening, she paused as a flicker of movement outside caught her eye. My God, someone else was out there. More than likely they'd been listening to her whole conversation with Inder-Jeet. Was Singh sending an army of spies to observe her?

Determined to confront this new threat head-on, Abby strode to the door. She wasn't sure what she had expected. It wasn't to find herself face-to-face with Mrs. Hamadi.

Abby's heart began to pound as she stood staring at the woman who'd stolen her child from the hospital. Dashing back to the hammock, she scooped up the baby and wrapped her arms around her tiny body.

Mrs. Hamadi regarded them wordlessly, but she didn't make any threatening movements. In the bright glare of the sun, she looked haggard. Deep circles were etched into the skin below her eyes, her flesh seemed thinner, older. And the red jewel in her nose was the only bit of color in her face. She looked as if she'd aged ten years since Abby had seen her in Baltimore.

With a quick glance at the guard, Mrs. Hamadi stepped just inside the door. She started to speak, and for a second Abby had trouble understanding what she was talking about.

"*She* did nothing for you. *I* got the diapers," she hissed. "And *I* got the formula she has been drinking."

"What?"

"*Inder-Jeet* had nothing to do with taking care of Shannon."

"And she didn't steal her, either," Abby managed as she took an involuntary step back.

"You hate me, don't you?"

"I—"

The woman's dark eyes turned liquid with deep regret. "I didn't come here to take your little one from you again."

"But why did you do it in the first place?" Abby choked out. "Why did you do that to us?"

The woman's features twisted. "I didn't have a choice."

"Of course you did. Everyone has a choice."

"No. Do you know the word *parai?*"

Abby shook her head.

"It means property. Human property. In this country, a woman belongs to someone else to do with as he pleases. Her father, then her husband. It can be a kind of slavery. But I think you wouldn't understand. No woman raised like you would understand."

Abby could only grip Shannon more tightly. In truth, she hardly did comprehend what she was hearing.

Perhaps Mrs. Hamadi saw the look of horror in her eyes, because she turned quickly away.

"Wait! I want you to explain it to me."

Instead of answering, the kidnapper turned and vanished into the desert heat.

NO MORE VISITORS came to the tent. Abby knew the Lion was keeping her isolated, as if to emphasize that she was entirely at his mercy in this wilderness encampment.

Every time the wind played with the flap of the tent, she looked up, hoping to see Steve come striding through the doorway. He didn't come. So she tried to occupy her mind by thinking about Mrs. Hamadi.

There was no denying she'd been angry at the woman. She was still angry—because Mrs. Hamadi was such a tangible focus for all the fury she'd stored up over the past week. But her own churning emotions and her surprise at seeing the kidnapper again had made her handle the encounter all wrong.

She'd been wishing for an ally in this godforsaken camp. Well, there was only one person besides Steve who seemed to understand what she'd been going through. And she'd driven her away.

Abby sighed; perhaps she'd get a second chance. If she saw Mrs. Hamadi again, she'd try to be gentler with the woman, try to make her believe that the two of them might help each other.

AN OLD WOMAN who said nothing and kept her face veiled brought a dinner of meat and vegetable stew and a large pitcher of tepid water and a basin. The water made Abby realize how gritty, uncomfortable, and sore she was.

She desperately needed a bath. But the thought of getting undressed made her feel too exposed. So she took off her clothing in stages—with one eye on the door and a towel within quick grabbing distance.

Her bag had been brought to the tent before she arrived. And Steve's, too. So he should be here soon, shouldn't he?

After putting on a loose-fitting shirt and shorts, she checked on Shannon again, which she'd probably been doing every ten or fifteen minutes. She had no real way of knowing how much time had passed. All at once it was almost impossible to contain her fears. Why didn't Steve come? Was he all right? Was Singh questioning him? Torturing him?

A shudder went through her frame, and she leapt up and started for the door of the tent. The moment she set foot outside, the guard was in front of her, his sword drawn. With a gasp, she stepped back, pulling the canvas flap tightly closed behind her. On a little groan of defeat, she dropped back onto the rug where she'd been sitting, closed her eyes, and tried to will her blood pressure down to some kind of normal level.

But she could still feel the pulse pounding in her temple as she huddled in the darkening tent.

More time passed, and fatigue began to win out over tension. Abby settled back against the rug and closed her eyes. The next thing she knew, she was blinking up into the glow of a lantern. A large hand grasped the light, and behind the circle of illumination, a shadowy figure loomed over her.

She gasped, and tried to back away.

"You were asleep. I'm sorry."

"Steve. Thank God." She was on her feet in one smooth motion, hurling herself into his waiting arms. He caught her, holding the lantern away from her with one hand while he clasped her tightly with the other.

"Easy. You don't want to burn the place down."

"I'm sorry. I'm just so glad to see you."

"Lord, yes." He held her possessively, his lips skimming her cheek, her hair. "Are you all right?"

"I am now."

"And Shannon?"

"We're both okay. But I've been worried about you," she blurted.

Steve's eyes were intent on her face, and he spoke slowly, as if trying to convey more than the substance of his words. "I was making arrangements with Singh."

Abby took a deep breath and tried to think before she gave too much away—to whoever might be outside. "His wife, Inder-Jeet, was here. She said she'd come to see if I had everything I needed, but she was really trying to find out if I knew where his precious merchandise is stashed."

"I hope you told her the truth. That I didn't tell you a damn thing about it because you were safer not knowing," Steve said very deliberately, his gaze burning into hers.

"Yes." The syllable came out as a little gasp. "That's what I told her."

She saw his wariness go down a notch.

"Good. Because it's dangerous to lie to a man as savvy as Amarjit Singh."

Abby nodded her agreement. They'd both taken a terrible chance—and their stories had matched.

Her gaze shot to the door of the tent.

Steve nodded almost imperceptibly. "Did they give you what you need to take care of Shannon?" he asked, as if domestic matters were uppermost on his mind.

"Yes." She gestured toward the hammock. "Come see her."

He walked slowly toward the bed and stood for several heartbeats gazing down at the sleeping child. When he reached out and touched her gently, she stirred and then began to whimper.

He jerked his hand back.

"I'm sorry. I—I woke her up."

"No," Abby assured him quickly. "She's been asleep for hours. It's probably time for her to eat. And she's wet."

She watched Steve watching her as she changed Shannon, washed her hands, and got out one of the bottles of milk from the carton. As she settled into the seating area, Shannon began to suck noisily. Steve hesitated for a moment, then sat down beside Abby, slinging his arm around her shoulders.

She moved over and rested her head against his shoulder. He was silent for several moments. Then he reached out to gently take hold of his daughter's foot,

stroking the soft baby skin. ''Would it be all right—?
Can I feed her?''

''Oh, Steve, of course.''

''How do I hold her?''

''The way I am. Just be sure to support her head.''

He made an awkward cradle of his arms, and she
settled Shannon into them.

His hand wasn't quite steady as he took hold of the
bottle. The baby stared up at him, her eyes large. But
she must have sensed the security of his grip because
she kept right on eating.

Steve wasn't quite as relaxed as his daughter. At first
he held himself stiffly, like a man who'd been handed
a priceless Venetian glass vase that might shatter at any
moment. Then as he got the feel of holding the baby,
he began to settle back more comfortably against the
rug. At the same time, Abby watched his features
change from anxious to incredibly soft and tender. If
there had ever been a father who loved his daughter, it
was this one.

''You're good with her,'' Abby whispered, her voice
catching a little. Tears misted her eyes, and she pressed
her cheek to Steve's shoulder. ''But I knew you would
be.''

He shifted Shannon more firmly against his muscular chest.

She'd always seen this man as the epitome of mas-
culinity. He was tough. Aggressive. Dangerous. Yet the
tiny baby looked so natural in his arms.

''I didn't realize how much I'd like holding her,'' he
said in a thick voice. ''How...much I'd...care about
her.''

Abby squeezed his arm.

''Thank you for giving me this.''

"I think we did it together," she said with a chuckle in her voice.

"I don't mean just making a baby. That was the easy part. I mean, giving me the chance to find out how much being a father could mean. It's not just the two of us anymore. It's the three of us."

"Oh, Steve. I knew it was going to be that way. I always knew." She tipped her face up, finding his lips. Automatically, their bodies shifted, and Shannon was cradled between them.

Steve groped for Abby's hand, and she knit her fingers with his. His lips were very close to her ear. "Abby, you and Shannon are getting out of here first thing tomorrow."

"Not without you."

"Sweetheart, I love you, and I've got to know the two of you are safe. That's the only way I'll be free to deal with Singh."

"I'd like that same feeling of security about you."

He didn't answer, and her heart leapt into her throat.

Chapter Fourteen

"I'm not leaving without you," Abby repeated. A few moments ago she'd felt so safe and secure in Steve's arms. Now he was telling her the three of them couldn't stay together.

His expression was fierce, but he confined himself to a harsh whisper. "As long as you're in this camp, Singh's got too much of a hold on me."

"Steve, I can't—"

He didn't let her finish the protest. "Shannon has to come first. She's too little to take care of herself, so one of her parents has to bring her home. And in this case it's got to be you."

Abby pressed her forehead against her husband's shoulder, willing herself not to break down. She'd never thought she'd live to see the day when Steve Claiborne would be giving her lessons in parenting.

But he was right. Shannon had needed her from those first frightening days in the hospital. Still, she'd never weighed her duty to her daughter against abandoning her husband in an enemy stronghold.

Between them, their child stirred. Automatically, Abby picked up the baby, held her against her shoulder, and rubbed her back. She was rewarded with a loud belch.

Steve's lips quirked. "I didn't know we had a secret weapon."

"She has a lot of talents."

"Yeah." Steve's face turned serious again as he delicately cupped his hand around the back of Shannon's little head. "Abby, remember how I felt when I couldn't save someone else I loved? My sister. Sharon. I failed her."

"Steve, we both felt that way. But there was nothing either one of us could have done."

"I shouldn't have left her on her own. I was all the family she really had, and I didn't realize how much she needed me."

"You couldn't," she insisted, knowing that nothing she said would ever change his feeling about the tragedy of Sharon Claiborne.

"Now I don't want to fail you. And Shannon. I can't live with that, too."

Abby's chest ached with the need to make him understand that the things he was saying about Sharon came pretty close to *her* feelings about *him*.

Leave him here. Impossible. But deep in her heart she knew he was right. They both had to put Shannon first. And any protest she voiced would make it harder for him to carry out his plans.

"I'll bring her home," she whispered.

"Thank you," he said in a low voice.

She nodded as she shifted the baby back into feeding position.

Steve handed her the bottle, and Shannon grabbed his finger.

"She's strong."

Oh God, and I have to be, too, Abby silently told herself.

Together they finished giving their child her midnight meal. Together they played with her, talked to her, exclaimed over the smiles she gave them. Together they changed her diaper again, and her tiny gown. The whole time, Abby was choked with emotions she dared not unleash. And every time she slid Steve a sideways glance, she could see he was keeping himself under the same kind of tight control.

She watched him take Shannon in his arms, his lips tenderly brushing back and forth against her cheek.

"She's so soft."

"Yes."

"She smells so sweet." He held her for several seconds longer before laying her in the hammock. His hand lingered on her back. "Before she was born, there was no way you could make me understand how much I was going to love her," he whispered.

Abby clasped her arm around her husband's waist. He looked like a man storing up impressions, sensations...feelings. Was he wondering if he'd ever see his child again?

The intensity of the moment was almost too much to take. Abby watched Steve shake himself and glance around the tent, as if he were disoriented. His gaze settled on the washbowl and pitcher.

"I'm still pretty gritty," he muttered.

"Oh, Steve, I wasn't thinking. You're probably feeling like a mess. But I used up most of the water." It was a relief to back off from her fears and focus on something uncomplicated.

"Yeah. But they'd better extend their gracious hospitality to both of us." Steve stepped to the door of the tent. "Bring more water," he demanded into the darkness.

He must have received an affirmative answer from the guard who'd been lurking around the door, because he stripped off his shirt, strode back to the basin and began to wash his hands. Minutes later, the guard returned with a second pitcher.

In the flickering light from the lantern, Abby watched him wet the cloth she'd used earlier and begin to sluice water over his neck and shoulders.

He threw back his head and inhaled deeply. "Damn, that feels good."

She drew in a deep breath and let it trickle from her lungs. Never before in her life had she realized how much simple pleasures could mean. "I thought so, too. Except that I kept being afraid someone might come in."

"Anyone I find lurking around this tent tonight is going to find himself ass-down in a sand dune," he said loudly enough for half the camp to hear.

Despite everything, she grinned at him.

And he grinned back. Then he stripped of the rest of his clothes, wet the cloth again, and began to work it across his broad chest.

Washing was such an intimate task, she thought. Really, she should give him some privacy. Yet it was impossible not to be drawn to the sight of her husband's nude body. It was too fascinating to observe the play of his muscles, the droplets of water glistening on his taut skin.

Her eyes followed the path of the cloth as it moved across his chest and down to his flat stomach. It was the same cloth she'd used. And in her mind she began to replace it with her hands.

She felt tiny jolts of sensation along her nerve endings as she imagined her palms and fingers on his firm flesh.

He looked up, his gaze skimming over her and coming to rest on her face.

She felt heat rise in her cheeks. "I—I'm sorry. I should let you have some privacy."

"That's okay. I think we can make the best of primitive conditions."

"You've missed a few spots."

"Where?"

"Your face. Let me help," she offered softly, moving toward him.

He pressed the cloth into her upturned palm. Abby dipped the rag into the cool water and wrung it out. Obligingly, he tilted his head. As she began to minister to him, his eyes stayed on her. She could feel the heat radiating from his body, see how he was responding to her, and her own temperature rose in answer. Gently she dabbed away the dried blood around the cuts on his forehead, his cheeks, and his chin. Her task was finished, yet she couldn't resist tracing the curve of his mouth with the damp cloth.

"That's better," she said, letting out a shaky breath.

"Much better," he agreed huskily as he began to dry himself.

"Steve—"

He stopped her before she could bring the conversation back to where they'd left it hanging. "Sweetheart, I don't want to talk about where we are, or that we're going to be separated tomorrow. I just want to love you."

Unable to deny him anything he asked, she opened her arms.

He came into them with a deep, shuddering sigh. Then he was holding her, kissing her, pressing her tightly to his body, sliding his hands urgently over her.

Even as her breath quickened and her skin began to glow with heat, she looked questioningly up at him.

He nodded in understanding before reaching for his duffel bag and pulling out a small plastic packet. "Abby, when I went out to get supplies for the trip, I bought these."

She took the condom out of his hand, clutching it tightly in her fist. "Trust a man to think of the essentials," she whispered.

Steve adjusted the lantern so that there was only the barest glow of light in the tent. Yet it was impossible not to see the need on his face as he turned back to her. She wanted to beg him to share whatever reckless plan he'd worked out. Instead, with a soft, yielding sound, she pressed the taut length of his body against hers.

"Oh, God, Abby, Abby," he growled. As his arms banded around her, he took her mouth in a devouring kiss. She responded with the same reckless urgency, lifting her lips from his only to land kisses on his cheek, his neck, his brows.

He did the same, his hands trembling as they tugged at her clothes. She felt the sheer power of their shared passion bind them tight and close.

Then, all at once, he stilled. "I don't want this to be like the first time we made love."

She swallowed. She had been remembering that time, too, but not regretfully. They'd been in a situation that had seemed as desperate as this, and they'd turned to each other just as they were doing now. "I don't understand," she managed.

"I was in too much of a hurry. I want to savor this, not rush through it."

"Steve, making love with you then was the most earth-shaking experience I'd ever had—bar none."

"Sweetheart."

"I just didn't know it was going to keep getting better and better."

He murmured more endearments, his voice low and husky as he took her down to the low bed. His hands were gentle but sensual as they trailed over her face, down her neck, and over the tops of her breasts.

"I love you. I love you so much." She sighed as his lips traced the same path, sending flames flickering over her skin. She'd never felt more erotically charged—or more frightened for the future. They'd both been thinking about the first time. Were they both afraid that this might be the last?

Abby pushed that terrible fear away and reached sensuously toward Steve, her lover, the father of her child, the man who had taught her so much about how to live each moment to the fullest. She wanted to savor their relationship. And she would. Not just tonight, but for the rest of their lives. Their long lives.

She clung to that affirmation, even as she looked into his eyes and trailed her fingers delicately down his chest, following the pace he had set, knowing that in this desert tent she would give him all the warm, sweet passion a woman could give the man she loved.

And she did.

STEVE CARESSED the side of her cheek, and Abby came instantly awake. She'd been dreaming they were back in their own bed in Baltimore. That they'd been making love long into the night... Well, the last part was true. But this wasn't Greenspring Valley.

Outside, the dawn was only a gray promise, but Steve was already dressed in the shorts he'd worn the night before and his remaining clean shirt.

When she stretched, the covers drifted to the tops of
her naked breasts. She shivered, as much from Steve's
heated gaze as from the chilly air.

She reached out, found his hand, and stroked his
fingers across her lips.

"You look very beautiful. And very tired," he said.

"Tired, anyway."

"I'm sorry."

"I'm not."

He settled down beside her. "I know it's early, and I
hate to wake you, but there are some important things
I've been putting off."

Abby nodded. She knew why he'd waited.

He leaned very close so that his words were barely
more than an exhalation. "I want you and Shannon
out of this camp as soon as possible. I don't want you
here if Singh brings the weapons back."

Abby sat up, feeling the blanket slip as she struggled
to frame the right question. "If he—" Before she could
finish the sentence, the tent flap was jerked aside like
a whip cracking in the dry desert air.

Steve sprang to his feet, whirling to face the entrance, his body in a defensive crouch. Abby shrank
back into the bed covers.

The intruder was Amarjit Singh.

"What the hell are you doing barging in to our
tent?" Steve demanded.

"Making your day, as you Americans say."

Abby could see Steve struggling to control his anger. "I thought early morning was for meditation."

"Unless circumstances dictate otherwise. It's time
for your wife to leave."

The raised voices of the two men awakened Shannon. The hammock in the corner began to sway, the
movement accompanied by a series of little cries.

Abby started to get up, remembered she was naked, and turned to Singh. "I need to take care of my baby, if you don't mind."

"The girl child can wait."

Shannon's whimper told Abby otherwise. She glared at Singh, then deliberately turned away. Draping the blanket like a toga around her body, she started toward the makeshift crib. But when she reached it, she realized there was no way she could both hold on to her covering and pick up a squirming infant.

Shannon, however, didn't understand the problem. She only knew she was hungry and uncomfortable. As soon as she saw Abby peering down over the side of the hammock, the cries grew louder, filling the tent like air expanding in a balloon.

"Your transportation will be ready to leave in fifteen minutes," Singh informed Abby, pitching his voice above the piercing wail.

She stood clutching her arms in front of her as much to hold herself together as to preserve her modesty. She was pretty sure the Lion was doing this deliberately. But why?

But that wasn't the worst part. Steve had been about to tell her something crucial. Now what were they going to do? "My daughter must eat. Would you mind leaving, so I can give her some breakfast?"

"You mean one of those bottles my wife insisted on ordering?" Singh sneered. "Was nursing her too much trouble for you, or were you afraid it would spoil your figure?"

Abby felt the blood drain from her face. "I did nurse her," she managed.

"But not now."

Her chin canted up. "Because you took her away from me," she said. "It's a bit difficult to maintain a milk supply when you're separated from your baby. Maybe Inder-Jeet will explain it to you, if you're interested," she said, tension stiffening her speech.

He had the grace to look away from her. Then he turned back to Steve. "You will come with me. We have some arrangements to finalize."

It would have been impossible to miss the threatening edge to his voice.

Yet Steve ignored the warning. "I believe my wife needs my help." Striding to the hammock, he bent down and picked up Shannon. She hiccuped. Then her cries diminished.

Cradling his daughter awkwardly in one arm, the man who had dealt with arms dealers, warlords and mercenaries from Calcutta to Canton got a bottle out of the carton and attached a nipple the way he'd seen Abby do it. When he inserted it into Shannon's mouth, she began to suck greedily.

"What? Are American men nursemaids? Is that why their wives like bottles of milk so much?" Singh asked.

Abby saw Steve's muscles tighten. At the same time, a look of anticipation flashed on the rebel leader's face. My God, was that it? Had he come here to provoke a confrontation? Was he hoping that an angry Steve Claiborne would slip and reveal important information before his wife could get out of the camp?

Under the circumstances, it wasn't a bad tactic.

Quickly, she crossed to her husband and extended the hand that wasn't gripping the blanket. "Darling, thank you for coming to our rescue," she said softly. "But I think I can manage now."

For several seconds, their eyes locked, and she tried to telegraph a warning. To her relief, she saw his fury subside. When he gave her a quick, cocky grin, she drew in a sigh of relief.

"We're wasting time," Singh broke in.

Steve handed Shannon to Abby, holding the blanket in place against her shoulder while she took her daughter. As he stepped closer, his head bent toward her ear. "Get away from him," he whispered. Or at least that was what she thought he said.

She grasped his arm for several seconds longer. Then he turned away and faced Singh.

"What did you want to discuss?"

"Come to my tent where we won't be interrupted by women's work."

IN FACT, it was almost an hour before Abby was allowed to leave. An hour in which she paced back and forth in her tent, stewing. Finally, two guards came to get her and made her stand for another ten minutes in the hot desert sun. She draped the blanket over Shannon's face and closed her own eyes, swaying slightly as she waited. Over and over she kept reminding herself of what she had to do.

She had to get out of here. With Shannon. She had to get her daughter to safety.

One of the guards barked a command. Another clasped Abby's arm and began to walk her forward.

Shannon started to cry as the wind from the blades hit her face, and Abby bent to cradle her daughter's small body with her own.

It took every ounce of willpower she possessed not to dig her heels into the sand. Somehow she kept walking. Steve wanted her out of the camp, and she knew he was taking terrible risks to make sure she got away. She owed it to him not to mess up his plans.

Two of the guards helped her up a set of pull-down metal steps. A woman followed her inside. Abby stared at her in surprise. It was Mrs. Hamadi.

Moments later the helicopter shuddered slightly and lifted them off into the air. Abby craned to look out the small rectangular window. The rebel camp dwindled away below them until it might have been a collection of tattered toy tents left out in a sandbox.

Several human figures were scattered among the rectangles of canvas. Abby wondered if one of them was Steve. Had he watched her board? Did he know she was actually on the plane?

His last urgent message echoed in her ears. "Get away from him." Whom did he mean? Or had she heard the word wrong. Had he really said "them"?

Abby's eyes swung to Mrs. Hamadi. She was sitting rigidly, as if the noise and the motion terrified her. Reaching across Shannon, Abby laid a hand over the other woman's.

"It's okay," she mouthed in the same tone she'd used to comfort Shannon, knowing it was impossible to hear anything above the noise of the motor and the baby's cries.

Mrs. Hamadi didn't move.

The wind was beginning to pick up, bringing back vivid memories of the earlier flight when they'd crashed in the sandstorm. Some of her tension dissipated as they left the blowing sand behind. Soon they were descending over a small airport. Abby searched the skyline and saw a concentration of taller buildings in the distance, which could have been New Delhi.

She began to think about an escape attempt as soon as they touched down. Surely there would be people around who could help her. But the ground crew stayed pointedly away from Singh's helicopter. The guard firmly escorted Abby to a car waiting at the edge of the airfield. And Mrs. Hamadi trailed obediently behind.

From there they drove several miles to a walled compound in what looked like a suburban area.

The house was comfortable, well appointed, and perfectly suited as a prison. As far as Abby could tell, there was only one entrance in the eight-foot wall that surrounded the grounds, and that was closed by a sturdy wooden gate.

The guard asked Abby to wait in the main hall, where several people dressed as servants kept her in full view. Although the men were wearing civilian clothes, their military bearing made Abby suspect that they were as handy with a rifle as a dust mop.

"In here, please."

Abby stepped into a small room.

Her fingers closed around the telephone receiver offered to her by the guard. "Hello?"

"Abby?"

She felt a surge of relief at the sound of Steve's voice. Then she realized he was probably in the communications tent, with Amarjit Singh standing beside him. He'd have to be careful about what he said. So would she.

"How are you?" she questioned, fighting to keep the quaver out of her voice.

"Fine. Abby, where are you?"

"At a house in—" She looked at the guard. "Where are we?"

"In New Delhi," the man clipped out.

Abby relayed the answer, feeling smug that she'd gotten the information.

"Good."

It was amazing how much Steve managed to convey with that one word.

"When are you joining me?" Abby questioned, holding her breath as she waited for the answer.

"I'm not sure. The wind is up."

"It was starting when I left." The last thing she wanted to discuss was atmospheric disturbances, yet she was willing to go through the weather report for the whole Indian subcontinent if it kept Steve on the phone. His voice was like a lifeline connecting the two of them.

"It's lucky you got away."

Hearing the double meaning in his words, Abby swallowed around the lump in her throat.

"I expect we'll hook up in Baltimore."

Abby felt as if the floor had dropped out from under her feet. Her knuckles turned white as they clamped around the receiver. "Steve, what are you telling me? Are you going with Singh to Oliver's?"

He ignored the question. "I'm sorry we didn't get a chance to say goodbye before you left," he continued. "Take care of Shannon. Give her a kiss for me."

"Steve, I love you," Abby choked out. She didn't care how desperate she sounded. She didn't care about anything but reaching across the miles to her husband.

"Yeah. Love you." She knew he was trying to sound as if he were just going down to the Royal Farm Store for a quart of milk. She knew he was doing that to fool Singh. Yet below the casually spoken words she heard the edge of regret in his voice. "Remember to do everything I told you."

There was a sharp click on the line.

"Steve? Steve? Wait!" Abby shouted into the receiver, her free arm clutching Shannon. The line had gone dead.

She turned quickly to the guard. "Can you get him back?"

"No." His eyes drilled into her. "If you want him to remain safe, you will cooperate. Come to your room, please, Mrs. Claiborne."

With numb fingers Abby set down the phone. *If you want him to remain safe,* her mind echoed the threat. Back at the desert camp, was Steve being given the same kind of warning about her?

On stiff legs, she followed her captor down the hall to a large, comfortably furnished bedroom. But she hardly noticed her surroundings, except for the grill-work barring the windows. When the door closed behind her, Abby sank to the edge of the bed, holding Shannon, rocking back and forth and trying desperately to work through the convoluted twists and turns of her situation—and Steve's.

Singh had transferred her from the desert encampment to a more comfortable prison. And after he picked up his strategic weapon, he could do anything he pleased with his hostages. Now Abby was dead certain he wasn't going to let them go, because the only way to make sure that word of his secret weapon never leaked out was to get rid of the Claibornes.

Steve had known all that. He'd wanted his wife and child out of the rebel camp, but he'd been anticipating a double cross, which was why he'd told her she had to escape. What's more, his own plans included another double cross—deadly exposure to Omega. The trouble was, it was going to be just as fatal for Steve as it was for Singh.

Abby moaned softly and clutched her baby to her breast. Steve had said Shannon came first. He'd meant *she* and Shannon.

His life for theirs.

But she couldn't let him go through with it. She had to think of a way to save him, and quickly. Before he and Singh arrived at the temple in the jungle.

Jumping to her feet, she started toward the door. This place had a phone line to the rebel camp. She could warn Singh about Omega. Only why should he believe her? And what if he did? Then he'd know Steve had lied, which would put all of them in a worse position.

The door on Abby's right opened, and she gave a little gasp. Then she tried to compose her face as Mrs. Hamadi stepped into the room. Struck anew by how haggard the woman looked, she waited to find out what she wanted.

"Do you need anything?" Mrs. Hamadi asked.

"I don't know yet. But thank you for coming to inquire."

As they regarded each other across Shannon's head, Abby tried to read the woman's expression.

"Why did you put your hand over mine in the helicopter?" Mrs. Hamadi asked suddenly.

"You were frightened. I wanted to help."

"Why should you want to help me?"

Abby felt a surge of cautious hope. Maybe, just maybe, she had found an ally. "I thought we could comfort each other."

Mrs. Hamadi looked down, as if studying the pattern of the rug. "I stole your child. You should hate me."

"It's Singh who deserves my anger—not you."

The other woman was silent for several seconds. "It would be dangerous for me to agree with you," she whispered.

Abby stepped close to her. "Is there somewhere we can talk?" she mouthed.

The older woman hesitated a long time. Abby held her breath, feeling as if her lungs would burst. Finally Mrs. Hamadi gestured for her to follow. They went through the adjoining room and then out another door. To her surprise, Abby found it led to a rectangular garden between the house and the wall.

"Mrs. Hamadi."

"That isn't my name. I am Mrs. Amarjit Singh."

"But Inder-Jeet—?"

"In our culture, a man may take another wife—if his first is barren." She raised her head and looked directly at Abby. "I lied to you all those weeks ago in Baltimore. I was telling you the story Singh wrote out for me. My husband didn't divorce me when I couldn't give him a child. Instead he made me endure the humiliation of seeing him bring another woman to his bed. Inder-Jeet is young, but she has already given him two sons."

"That must be hard for you."

"I told you, I am *parai*. Property. I should be grateful I was allowed to continue in the household of such a great man."

"You . . . you admire him?" Abby choked out.

"Not for the way he treats me. But he is a symbol for our people. They call him the Lion. And they follow him."

Abby felt her hopes die. Asking for Mrs. Hamadi's—no, Mrs. Singh's—help could be fatal.

The woman's gaze flickered to the baby cradled protectively in Abby's arms and then to her face. "But I don't want to lie to you again. Not after I caused you so much anguish. And not after you made such a dangerous journey to get your little one back."

Abby tried to remain impassive as Mrs. Singh continued. "I did something very bad. I kidnapped your baby because I thought it might bring me back into my husband's favor." Her face contorted. "But I still mean nothing to him. That is making me sad—and angry. It is also making me think about the goals of Amarjit Singh. He claims to be fighting for freedom and justice for our people. But I don't believe he means this for our women. It is only the men who are important enough to be free."

"I'm sorry," Abby said.

"You don't know how lucky you are being born in a country where women are equal."

"Not perfectly equal," Abby demurred. "But we're getting there."

"There's another way you're lucky. You have a husband who loves you," Mrs. Singh continued in a low voice. "I was listening to some of what the men were saying yesterday. I know your husband is putting himself in danger by staying with the Lion. I know how hard he fought to get you sent away from camp. But if I were your husband, I wouldn't trust mine."

Abby took her lower lip between her teeth. Mrs. Singh had given her an opening. Or had she been sent here to get information, as Inder-Jeet had the night before? Abby knew that for her own safety and Shannon's, she shouldn't rush in to anything. Yet the longer she waited, the less chance she had of saving Steve.

Before she could decide what to do, Mrs. Singh began to speak again. "I was brought up in a religious home," she said. "I was taught to revere the teachings of Guru Nanak and the other wise men. And I tried to be a good woman. I think I was a moral person—" She stopped abruptly. "When I got to know you in the hospital, I could see how much you loved your baby, how devoted you were. Then I stole her from you.

Since that day my mind is very troubled. I do not sleep.
I do not eat.''

"What do you want from me?"

To Abby's consternation, Mrs. Singh went down on
her knees in front of her. "Forgiveness."

Abby put a hand on the other woman's shoulder.
Both of them were trembling. "There is a condition on
my forgiveness," she managed.

"What?"

"Help us get away."

"You ask the impossible."

Abby watched in dismay as Mrs. Singh scrambled up
and fled toward the house.

Chapter Fifteen

Steve stood listening to the wind, feeling the tent sway around him as sand battered the canvas sides. The storm was getting stronger. With any luck it would pick up to hurricane force and sweep this whole damn camp into oblivion.

He allowed himself to picture tents, men, camels and supplies cartwheeling off into a five-hundred-foot dune. Everything swept away—except Steve Claiborne, who would somehow walk back into town and tell his wife everything was okay.

He sighed and turned toward the interior of the shelter, his eyes focusing on the small hammock that still stood near one wall—and the bed where he and Abby had spent the night in each other's arms.

The memory of her whispered words of love and her sweet kisses made him momentarily light-headed. Then he recalled her desperate voice on the phone a few hours ago, and his face contorted. He'd deliberately withheld information from her so she couldn't interfere with his plans.

"Abby, I'm sorry," he murmured, so low that the words were lost under the roar of the wind. Two nights ago, after the plane crash, he'd vowed that he was going to get her and Shannon out of danger if it was the last thing he did.

He hoped it wouldn't come to that. "I'm doing the best I can—for all of us. I'm trying to make it work out right," he whispered. "But if you never see me again, please try and remember I love you more than anything else in the world."

WAS SHE UNDER house arrest, the way she had been in the tent? Or could she go out into the garden by herself? Abby wondered. Prowling around the bedroom, she found a fancy English perambulator in the closet. With Shannon inside, she started down the hall.

When she saw the guard who'd come with her from the camp, she stopped for a moment, then continued on, acting as though she had a perfect right to take her daughter for a walk in the sunshine. The guard looked confused, as if he couldn't believe a woman had challenged the Lion's authority. He opened his mouth and closed it again.

Abby ignored him as he followed several paces behind her. She pushed the pram up a brick path, pretending an absorbing interest in the landscaping, but she was really looking at the high, smooth wall, trying to figure out how to get over it. There were no handholds, and she was beginning to suspect there wasn't a chance in hell of escaping when she came to a section planted with a stout vine that looked as if it would hold her weight. But there was no way to find out for sure without trying.

Sticking with her ambling pace, she toured the garden for another ten minutes but didn't see any better alternatives. Then she headed back to her bedroom, her mind in turmoil.

It was one thing for her to assume the risk of getting shot in the back. But what about Shannon? Was it possible to climb over the wall encumbered by a baby? What if Shannon slowed her down? What if they fell?

Shannon began to fuss. Abby scooped her up and sank into the rocking chair by the window, her hands tender and possessive on her daughter as she began to feed her.

"Oh, Shannon," she murmured, rocking back and forth, feeding her daughter, stroking her soft skin. She'd never felt more torn apart. The only thing she knew was that under cover of darkness she was going to break out. Or there was no hope for Steve.

Holding Shannon tightly, she stole toward the window. The ornamental grillwork had probably been intended to protect the woman who lived in this room, not to jail her. It was secured with inside screws. How hard would it be to remove them?

Abby laid the baby on the bed and then pawed through the contents of the dressing table and found a metal nail file. Working quickly, she loosened one screw, then another. To her surprise and relief, it took only a few minutes to detach the grill. After propping it back into place, she pulled the curtains almost closed and stood back. No one would know what she'd done unless they actually yanked on the bars.

Which probably wouldn't happen. Singh's guards wouldn't think that a mere woman would have the gumption to put an escape plan into action. In fact, their low opinion of womanhood was probably the best thing she had going for her, Abby decided as she lay down beside Shannon on the bed, curling herself defensively around her tiny body.

Already asleep, the infant snuggled up against her mother's tummy. But Abby was too distraught to do more than doze. Every so often she glanced at the window, seeing the shadows lengthening and feeling her dread increase.

Finally she fell into a troubled sleep—and was caught almost immediately in the grip of a nightmare. She, Shannon, and the woman she still thought of as Mrs. Hamadi were back at the desert camp. Guards were holding her and Mrs. Hamadi by the arms as the two of them tried frantically to reach Shannon's crib. But they couldn't break free. And Amarjit Singh was standing over the baby holding a knife. Then Steve was there, too, held by another guard behind the crib. A guard who pressed a knife to his throat.

Abby woke with her heart pounding and her skin clammy. With a strangled sob, she folded her daughter close.

Scrambling up, she ran to the closet where she'd seen several folded saris on shelves. With shaky hands, she ripped the ends of one apart, making straps that she could tie around her neck and waist to make a baby carrier. Then she found a purse with a shoulder strap into which she could stuff some diapers and bottles.

She was about to secure Shannon to her chest when there was a loud knock on the door. Abby stuffed the sari under the pillows and called out "Come in."

A female servant entered, carrying a tray of food. "Your dinner."

"Thank you," she said, hoping her voice sounded normal. "I—I'll put the tray outside when I finish." She'd almost made a terrible mistake. What if she'd already left, and the woman had found her gone?

Realizing she was starving, Abby wolfed down a flat bread stuffed with potato and onion while she fed Shannon again. Then she tied her daughter into the makeshift carrier. Unaccustomed to the sling, the baby began to whimper.

"Honey, please don't cry now," Abby soothed, looking through the baby supplies for a pacifier. There wasn't one. "If you make noise, they'll catch us."

Finally, Shannon quieted. But for how long? Knowing the baby was the weak link in her escape plan, Abby slung the purse with the diapers and bottles over her shoulder. Then she crossed to the window and set the grill on the floor.

She was pushing up the sash as quietly as she could when a hand on her shoulder made her freeze.

Whirling, she found herself facing Mrs. Singh.

"I knew you would do this," the older woman said. "I knew you would not bow to the Lion's wishes."

"Please. Let us go," Abby gasped.

"I will do better than that. I will help you."

"But you said—"

"Yes. For the guard. He came up around the corner of the building while we were talking. You couldn't see him, but I knew he was listening."

Abby stared at Mrs. Singh, trying to read her expression, trying to determine whether this was really a trick to give the guards an excuse to kill their prisoner.

"They will check your bed in the night. I will be in it with the covers pulled up around my face. And this will be in the crib." She unwrapped a bundle she'd been holding.

Stupefied, Abby found herself looking at a large baby doll dressed in clothes similar to the ones Shannon was wearing.

"Go," Mrs. Singh repeated. "We are in a suburb of New Delhi. Go straight down the road from the back of the house. In four blocks you'll come to a shopping area. There will be cabs.'' As she spoke, she pressed a wad of bills into Abby's hand.

''What will they do to you?'' Abby managed.

''Nothing. I will be back in my own bed before morning. No one will think that I would dare betray the Lion. It is the guard who will get into trouble. Singh will think he didn't check on you.''

''Why are you helping us?''

''To ease my conscience. And because I know I have caused a good woman terrible grief. Now leave. Quickly. The man from the camp is having his dinner in the kitchen. This is the best time for you to escape.''

''I— Thank you.''

The two women looked at each other. Abby reached for Mrs. Singh's hand and squeezed it tightly. Then she shoved the money into her pocket and scrambled through the window. As soon as she was on the other side, Mrs. Singh replaced the grill.

The bending motion jiggled Shannon, and she whimpered. Abby froze. ''Please, please, honey,'' she murmured. ''Please.'' She pressed the edge of her hand against her daughter's mouth, and Shannon began to suck. Abby sighed in relief.

After her eyes had adjusted to the dark, she tiptoed across the courtyard and around the house to the spot where she'd found the vine that afternoon. As she eased her hand out of Shannon's mouth, she held her breath. But the baby remained mercifully silent.

Grabbing the vine with both hands, Abby began to pull herself up. The pocketbook full of baby supplies flapped against her side, and she considered abandoning it. But that would be a dead giveaway. Besides, she couldn't afford any replacements at the moment.

Hours seemed to pass as she made her slow way toward the top of the wall, feeling for one handhold or

foothold and then another in the darkness. The farther she got from the ground, the more spindly the
stalks grew. She was six or seven feet in the air when
one of the branches gave way under her foot and she
fell several inches. Somehow she gagged her scream.
Somehow she found another foothold. Recovering with
a shuddering breath, she pressed her face against the
rough surface of the wall.

But the sudden movement had jarred Shannon, and
she started to whimper again. Awkwardly Abby leaned
into the foliage. Wrapping one arm around a swaying
stalk, she used her other hand to find her daughter's
mouth.

"Honey, please," she prayed. "Don't give us away.
Please."

Below her, a door opened and she heard footsteps on
the path. Every nerve in her body jumped, yet she kept
from twisting around and looking down.

Was it the guard? Had he heard Shannon? Would he
look up and see them? She waited tensely, expecting a
bullet to slam into her back.

The man below her called out harshly in the darkness.

Abby felt the air solidify in her lungs as she pressed
her hand more firmly to Shannon's mouth, feeling her
daughter's eager sucking.

Aeons passed. Finally the footsteps receded, and
Abby sagged limply against the vine. She wanted to
scramble upward toward freedom. She forced herself
to wait while she counted slowly to two hundred.

There were no sounds from below, so she began to
climb again.

At last she was at the top. With one more strong effort, she pulled herself onto the flat ledge. Every muscle in her body ached. She longed to rest and catch her

breath, but as she looked back into the compound, she knew this was the time of greatest danger. She was exposed like a target in a shooting gallery. Anyone who glanced outside could see her silhouetted against the night sky.

With gritted teeth, she began to lower herself to the other side. But the vine extended only a little way over the edge. Legs dangling, she pushed away from the wall, hitting the ground with a thud.

Shannon shrieked in alarm, but Abby couldn't stop to comfort her daughter. Cradling the infant's head, she dashed down the alley, afraid to stop until she'd put most of a block between herself and her prison.

Finally, lungs burning and muscles shrieking, she slowed to a walk and listened intently. To her profound relief, she heard no pursuing footsteps.

IT WAS JUST getting dark when one of the guards came for Steve. Hoping his tension didn't show, he stepped briskly into the Lion's den. The wind had died down a bit. Would Singh gamble on a takeoff under dangerous conditions? Steve didn't know, but he couldn't help thinking that if they crashed, that might be the best thing for Abby and Shannon.

"Well? Are you going to risk it?"

Singh eyed him appraisingly. "I think we both know the weather's still too uncertain. We'll try first thing in the morning."

Steve nodded, as if the timetable didn't make any difference to him.

"I want to firm up our plans. Give me the coordinates of the hideout."

"When we're in the air," Steve said easily.

The rebel leader glared at him. "Tell me now."

"If you know where you're going, you don't need me any longer."

"And you're hoping that if I have to bring you along, you'll have a chance to escape." Singh's voice had turned dangerous.

"No, I'm hoping that you'll be so pleased with our working relationship that we'll be able to continue the association," Steve shot back, wondering if Singh believed him. But it didn't matter. He still held the trump card. The Lion had to play this game by his rules.

"By the way, I wouldn't advise going in there by helicopter, if that's what you're planning," he continued.

"Why not?"

"Gibbs didn't use them, so you would be too conspicuous. Your birds don't have enough cargo space, anyway."

"What would you suggest?"

"Transferring to a plane."

"Transferring will waste time," Singh shot back.

"I'm giving you my best advice," Steve said impassively.

After a thirty-second silence, Singh agreed. "At least tell me which airstrip to contact so I can have this plane ready. And give me an idea of the range."

"Fair enough." Steve studied a map and pointed to a location. "Gibbs's hideout isn't more than two hours from here. But it's not marked on any charts, so you won't find it on your own. Even if you could, the cargo isn't in a warehouse."

"All right. You've made your point."

Steve stood and stretched. "Good. If you don't need me any longer tonight, I'd like to get some sleep." He turned and strode from the tent, knowing he'd bought himself—and Abby—an extra seven or eight hours.

THE SAFEST THING for Abby would have been to take refuge at the American consulate. Only that would have meant too many explanations—and too many delays. So she headed for the only place she knew in the city, the hotel where she'd met Steve after she'd flown out from Baltimore. Was that only ten days ago? It might have been a lifetime.

She quickly got a room, explaining she'd lost her purse and referring the clerk to the credit card impression she'd used the first time. Then she asked the international operator to phone Jason. His answering machine said all messages were being taken at another number. *Her* number. Puzzled, she called her own house. To her surprise, Erin Morgan answered.

"Abby, thank God. The last we knew, your plane went down. Where are you?"

"At the hotel where I met Steve last week."

"Did you get the baby?" Erin's voice was tense.

"Yes."

"Thank God," her friend repeated.

"But Steve is still in the rebel camp, and I need to talk to Jason."

"Oh, no! Abby, I'm sorry. Jason's not here."

Her hopes plummeted. Since she'd started working out escape plans, she'd been counting on Jason to help her save Steve.

"He and Noel left for India right after Steve called from Hong Kong."

"Here? They came here?" Her emotions took another wild swing. "How . . . how do I get in touch with them?"

"Jason left a number. It's for a Dr. Sunduram."

Somehow that was too much. Abby collapsed backward into her chair.

"What happened? Is everything all right?" Erin questioned urgently.

"I'm fine. And Shannon's fine." Abby tried to continue, but her voice broke. "I need Jason to help me rescue Steve," she finally managed. "Let me get off so I can call Dr. Sunduram."

"Yes. And, Abby, good luck."

"Thanks."

However, the doctor's number was busy. And it stayed busy for the next twenty minutes.

In between calls, Abby sat rigidly on the bed, feeling like a pressure cooker that was about to explode. Finally, in frustration, she phoned the lobby. "I need a cab to take me to a village a couple of hundred miles from here," she told the clerk at the desk.

"Tonight?"

"Yes."

"I'm sorry. I don't know if that can be arranged."

"Tell the driver I'm willing to pay a great deal of money for the service."

"Yes, miss. I think we can help you, miss."

Abby hung up and shuffled through the bills she still had left. It wouldn't be enough to pay an ordinary cab fare. Jason would just have to take care of it when she arrived at Dr. Sunduram's. If he was really there.

IT WAS FOUR in the morning when Abby stumbled up to Raj Sunduram's house, a sleeping Shannon in her arms. The door opened on her second knock.

Noel Zacharias answered. For a second she looked at Abby in disbelief. Then she held out her arms.

"Abby! Oh, Abby. Thank God. You've got Shannon! When your plane went down, we didn't know if you were alive or dead." She looked expectantly over Abby's shoulder. "Where's Steve?"

"Still with the rebels."

"Oh, Abby—"

"I need to talk to Jason," she interrupted.

"He's in town. Raj got a call about Oliver's body this evening, and they went to the medical examiner's office—or whatever it's called around here. I can't understand why they haven't come back."

"I've got to tell him—"

"After you are paying your cab fare, missus."

The gruff voice of the driver made Abby straighten. "Noel, do you have any money?"

"You mean, rupees? Not much."

The driver grabbed Abby's arm. "I am taking you all the way out here in the middle of the night. You are paying or I call the police!"

Abby tried to wrench away. "I'm not trying to cheat you. You'll get your money."

"Will you take dollars?" Noel asked.

"How many dollars?"

THE CONTINGENT from the rebel camp took off before first light, heading north by northwest to the airstrip Steve had designated the night before. There they changed to a fifteen-passenger plane.

Singh took the controls and Steve sat in the copilot's seat. Three armed guards were the only passengers. The rest of the seats were folded out of the way to make a cargo bay. Not until they'd been flying for twenty minutes did he give the rebel leader the coordinates for Gibbs's landing strip.

"I know the area. I should have looked there," Singh growled.

"You could look from now till Gurū Nānak's birthday. I told you the cargo's not in a warehouse. I hope you're up for a trek into the jungle."

"Where in the jungle?"

"We'll discuss that when we get there."

Singh gave him a dark look before turning his attention to the controls.

Steve leaned back and tried to relax. There was nothing he could do for the moment. But he couldn't stop worrying about Abby and Shannon.

"NOEL, I'VE GOT to understand what's going on. How long have you been here? And why did you and Jason come?" Abby asked urgently.

"Steve asked Jason to decontaminate the shipment. We've been here a little more than forty-eight hours."

The air rushed out of Abby's lungs. "Did he do the decontamination? Is it safe to go near the temple?" Her heart skipped a beat and then started pounding in double time as she waited for the answer.

"I—I don't know. They were working on it, then they got the message from the medical examiner and hurried off."

"Was the medical examiner calling about the poison in Oliver's body? Is it worse than we thought?"

Noel fluttered her hands in frustration. "I wish I knew. Jason and Raj picked up his medical records and tore out of here in a terrible flap. I guess they thought they could fill me in when they got back. We weren't expecting you."

Abby closed her eyes and tried to think. She felt as if she were trapped in a maze and every path turned out to be a dead end. She sucked in a steadying breath and let it out slowly. "Okay. I'll have to assume it's still not safe to go into the temple," Abby murmured as she stood up. "Is there a car I can use? And a gun?"

Noel didn't answer.

"I'm sure Jason would have left a gun with you," Abby enunciated carefully. "Where is it?"

"I'm sorry, yes." Noel scrambled up and hurried down the hall to the bedroom Steve and Abby had used. In a few moments she was back with an automatic pistol and several extra ammunition clips.

Abby emptied out the purseful of baby supplies and stowed the weaponry. "What about transportation?" she asked.

"They took Raj's Jeep, but our rental is here."

"Good. I've got to get to the temple before Steve and Singh."

"Let me come with you."

Abby shook her head. "No. You've got to stay with Shannon."

"But what can you do by yourself?"

"I don't know." She nuzzled her lips against her daughter's cheek. God, how she wanted to stay here and wait for Jason and the doctor to get back. But that might be too late. With a leaden feeling in her chest, she handed the sleeping child to Noel.

Her friend clutched the infant awkwardly. "I think I know more about handling a pistol than a baby."

Abby laughed and gestured toward the supplies she'd dumped out on the couch. "You'll get the hang of it real fast." She swallowed. "And . . . and if something bad happens, love her for me."

"Nothing's going to happen to you!"

"I hope not."

"I'm going to see if I can get in touch with Jason." Noel was obviously struggling to keep her voice steady.

"Thanks. Tell him where I've gone."

Abby backed away. She wanted to reach out and snatch Shannon to her breast. Instead she turned and fled.

THE SUN was just streaking the eastern sky pink as Abby headed down the road toward Oliver's compound. The dawn's early light, she mused as she stepped on the accelerator.

She pulled in at the airstrip, half afraid she was going to find a plane on the runway. But the place was dark and deserted. Quickly she drove to the warehouse and found the key where Steve had hidden it. Inside she looked around and located a stack of crates she remembered from their earlier visit. The contents were probably intended for guerilla warriors or terrorists. She'd never thought of herself as either, but she knew the only way to fight Amarjit Singh was by his own rules.

Twenty minutes later, she was a lot better supplied. Briefly she considered making her stand right where she was. Singh would have to land here, wouldn't he?

But that wasn't certain. If he came by helicopter, he could go directly to the temple.

After locking the door, she jumped back into her borrowed Jeep and roared up the hill, heading for the road into the jungle.

DAYLIGHT HAD BARELY broken when the small plane circled the airstrip several times and then came in for a landing. After cutting the engine, Singh climbed out and inspected the deserted facility.

He gestured toward the warehouse. "Let's have a look in there."

"I thought you were in a hurry to pick up your merchandise."

"Maybe I'll find something else I can use."

Steve shrugged and jumped down to the hard-packed dirt, conscious of the guard right behind him. If Singh wanted to delay, that was fine with him.

The rebel leader was already rattling the steel-reinforced door of the warehouse. Before Steve could produce the key, Singh pulled out an automatic pistol and shot off the padlock. Inside he began to inspect the stacks of crates. "It appears I'm not Gibbs's only disappointed customer," he called over his shoulder.

"I wouldn't know."

"I think we'll take some of this with us to the camp."

"Be my guest."

Singh crossed to a crate that lay open on the floor surrounded by straw packing material. "Someone's been messing with this stuff."

Steve stared into the open box.

"Who's been here? Was that box open before?"

"I don't remember."

"I think you would," Singh returned, his eyes narrowed. Drawing the gun again, he pointed it at Steve. "I think you'd better show me that other hiding place. The one that's supposed to be in the jungle."

ABBY WAS HALFWAY UP the narrow track when she heard a small plane coming in for a landing.

At least it wasn't a helicopter. At least they weren't going to beat her to the temple. Her overwhelming impulse was to speed ahead so she'd be in position soon as possible. Instead she made herself ease up on the accelerator. The foliage would soon be too dense to drive through, but she couldn't leave the Jeep on the road. If Singh saw it, he'd wonder who else was snooping around the temple. Which could be fatal—both to herself and Steve.

Anxiously, she scanned the greenery, looking for a place to ditch her transportation. At the next break in the trees, she nosed into the underbrush. Small limbs slapped against the sides and windshield, making it almost impossible to see where she was going, but she was able to ease forward for several yards. Finally the bumper jolted against something solid, and she came to a rattling stop.

After climbing out and pushing her way out to the road, she looked back toward the Jeep. It was barely visible. Which should do, unless Singh was expecting trouble.

Her fingers tightened around the bag with the loot she'd taken from the warehouse. Whatever happened now, she wasn't going to turn back. Maybe the temple was really decontaminated, she told herself. Maybe that was why Steve was risking coming here. But even if that were true, he was still in danger. As soon as Singh and his men had what they wanted, they'd probably shoot Steve.

Abby clenched her teeth as she trotted up the road. The same deadly stillness hung heavy in the air like mist rising from a graveyard. Her eyes darted to the yellow and brown leaves, dangling as limp as spider webs. Had the poisoned area spread? Either there was more destruction since they'd been here, or she'd been closer to the temple than she realized when she nosed the Jeep off the road.

The place had the smell of pestilence about it, and Abby tried to breathe shallowly. She also kept her eyes away from the limp gray shapes partially hidden by the leaves.

The sight of the temple rising out of its circle of death brought her to a halt. Now she could feel an acid sting of the air every time she took in a breath. Forcing herself to put one foot in front of the other, she walked forward until she could see the entrance. It loomed like a portal to the underworld—dark and forbidding—at the front of the ancient building.

Abby was trying to figure out the best place to conceal herself when the noise of a car's engine broke the lethal silence.

My God. She didn't have much time. They were already coming up the road.

Panicked, she lunged into the underbrush, feeling the brown leaves slap and scrape at her bare legs as she waded forward. Ignoring the stinging sensation, she kept moving. A five-foot-high pile of stones seemed to offer the best cover. Scrunching down, she turned back in the direction from which she'd come.

All her attention was focused on the approaching vehicle, which was why the gun barrel thrust into the middle of her back made her gasp in startled shock.

"Raise your hands. Then turn around very slowly."

Even through her own fear, Abby caught the edge of hysteria in the man's voice. If she didn't do exactly what he said, she was going to be killed.

The bag dropped from her fingers and her hands went up. When she turned to face her captor, she felt her mouth gape open.

It couldn't be. But it was.

"Oliver? Oliver Gibbs?" she croaked.

Chapter Sixteen

"Abby? Steve's wife?" Oliver Gibbs stared at her with the same incredulity she knew was plastered on her own face.

"Don't shoot," she wheezed.

Steve's former partner moved the machine gun he held to the side.

Abby tried to take in details that would add up to an explanation. His skin was pale and damp, his eyes were sunken in their sockets, and his clothing was wrinkled and stained. He looked ill and disheveled, but this wasn't a scene from *The Night of the Living Dead*.

He continued to gaze back at her as if he still wasn't sure he was face-to-face with Abby Franklin. And some corner of her mind acknowledged that she probably didn't look much like the well-groomed, relaxed woman he'd met in New Delhi.

"What the hell are you doing here?" he demanded.

"We found a dead man. In your bed," Abby managed.

"Ari. He brought Tang Wu's cargo in from Hong Kong. It was poison, wasn't it? Wasn't it?" Oliver plowed on without waiting for an answer. "He was sick, out of his head. He begged me to kill him. I couldn't do it. But I gave him the gun." The weapon in

Oliver's hand jerked, and Abby pressed back against the rock.

"The cargo was poison," he repeated.

"Yes."

"That bastard Wu pulled a fast one on me. He set me up with boxes of stuff that were going to kill me—after I'd put down a stiff deposit."

"No. I think his Russian source didn't pack the Omega properly." She swallowed. "Why was Ari in your bed?"

"I put him there. I fooled you, didn't I? I saw the look on your face when you turned around. You thought I was dead. Only I wasn't expecting you, I was expecting Wu's men. Or Singh's."

They were barely communicating, and Abby wondered how much exposure he'd gotten. Had Omega damaged his brain cells? "Please, we don't have much time," she tried to get through to him. "I've got to tell you why I'm here."

"God, I shouldn't have come back. But I thought it was safe."

"Where were you?"

"Hiding." He laughed. "In a cave I found up in the hills. It's not plush, but it's secure."

The engine noise from the road quit abruptly.

"Who's coming?" Oliver questioned, his voice quavery. "Is it Steve?"

"Yes. But he's with Singh."

Gibbs cursed low and vehemently.

"Do you know what's happened? About our baby?" she asked quickly. She wanted to beg for his help, but in his present condition, she'd be lucky if Oliver didn't get in the way.

"Steve. A father. I can't believe it."

"Singh didn't know where to find you. When he didn't get his merchandise, he thought Steve could deliver the shipment." Abby struggled to compress vital information. "He kidnapped our little girl and held her for ransom. That was ten days ago. Singh let me take Shannon out of the rebel camp, but he hung on to Steve."

Oliver's face turned grayer. "Oh, Jesus. I was going to make a lot of money. Pay off the debt I owed Steve. Buy more planes. But everything's gone wrong, hasn't it?" Raising the gun again, he swung around in the direction of the road.

"Don't." Abby struggled to control her voice. She'd dealt with enough unstable patients to realize there was no way of telling what Oliver Gibbs would do. "Please, they've got Steve."

The words were barely out of her mouth when Steve and Singh came into view on the narrow road. Her husband was in the lead. Singh walked slightly in back of him, a machine gun cocked under his arm. Bringing up the rear were three guards, also carrying automatic weapons.

"Too many. We haven't got a chance." Oliver sank down onto one of the rocks. The gun slipped from his grasp, and he cradled his head in his trembling hands.

Abby held her breath as the party approached the temple. She was reaching her hand into the bag she'd brought when Steve stopped and gestured toward the darkened doorway. "Your death shipment is in there. Before you get your hands on it, answer a question. How many people do you have to kill to accomplish your goals?"

Singh shrugged. "How many? Does it matter? I'm going to pick a city and wipe it out. That's the only way the government will pay attention."

"A city? You mean hundreds of thousands of people? But every one you kill is a tragic loss to someone else. Husbands will mourn wives. Parents, children. Whole families will be wiped out. You want that on your head?"

"I didn't bring you here for a lecture on morality," Singh snapped. "I'm trying to save *my* people. I can't think in terms of individuals who have despised us for generations."

"What if you're talking about your own death?"

"I've been prepared for that since the beginning."

"Good," Steve continued. "Because you're about to put your principles to the test. The poison you've come to get wasn't packaged properly. That's why Gibbs didn't deliver it—it killed him."

"No."

"Look at the dead vegetation around you. And listen. Do you hear anything moving? Have you heard anything but your own footsteps since we got out of Gibbs's Rover?"

Beside Abby, Oliver moaned. With her attention riveted to Steve, she'd forgotten all about the man who'd come back from the dead. Quickly she crouched and covered his mouth with her hand, praying that Singh hadn't heard.

Oliver yanked away from Abby's grasp and peered around the edge of the stones. She looked frantically from him to the scene on the road.

Singh had taken a step back from the door of the temple.

"Maybe if you leave now, you won't get a fatal dose," Steve grated. "But I wouldn't count on it."

"You're lying! You've lied to me every step of the way, haven't you? For a girl child. And a woman!" the Lion spat out. "What kind of man are you?"

"A man who loves his wife and daughter."

"If the Omega is going to kill *me*, what about you?"

Steve shrugged. "Like you, I've been prepared for that from the beginning."

Singh stared at him. Then, as if he were acting against his own will, he turned to peer into the lifeless jungle. So did his men. As soon as the gun was pointed the other way, Steve dived through the door of the temple and disappeared into the darkness.

"It's a trick. The son of Satan tricked me!" With a howl of rage, the rebel leader began to fire into the doorway. The other men followed suit.

Beside her, Oliver scrambled to his feet, but he was only a blur at the edge of Abby's vision. Praying that he wouldn't get in her way, she reached into the supply bag she'd brought. Her fist closed around what felt like a molded metal pineapple.

A grenade.

It was one of half a dozen she'd taken from the carton in the storage building. She'd already had a good look at the firing mechanism. It was simple enough to use. You just yanked out the pin, like in an old John Wayne movie.

She'd planned to toss it into the jungle, to convince Singh he was under attack and draw his attention away from Steve. She hadn't considered it as an offensive weapon—not with her husband standing next to the rebel leader.

But Steve had turned her hastily devised plan on its head. Instead of drawing Singh's attention, she had to stop him from going into the temple.

Teeth clenched, she pulled the pin from the grenade, astonished that it was so easy. You were supposed to count to five before throwing it. At least that's the way it worked in the movies.

One. Two. Three.

Abby felt each second tick by as an agony of lethal anticipation. She didn't get any further than three. With as much force as she could manage, she lobbed the grenade into the clearing in front of the temple and crouched—just as Oliver began to fire his weapon.

"It's me you want, you bastards!" he yelled as he sprayed the clearing with bullets.

"No!" Abby shouted, but he lurched around the side of the wall, still firing.

She didn't dare poke her head above the protective barrier. Not when the detonation was only seconds away.

All her muscles tensed as she waited, listening as Oliver's machine gun joined the clatter of the other weapons. Bullets sprayed the rocks in front of her as Singh's gunmen whirled around and fired back.

Then the weapons fire was cut off in mid-burst by an explosion that shook the ground, sending a deadly hail of shrapnel slashing into tree trunks, pinging off stones, tearing through leaves. It seemed to go on forever. Perhaps it lasted only a few seconds.

One moment the jungle was alive with the sounds of battle, then everything was as deathly quiet as the first time she and Steve had come up the road.

"Steve?" Abby called out as she drew the gun from the waistband of her shorts and peered from behind the wall of rocks. "Steve?"

Shuddering, she looked at the bodies on the ground. The rebels were near the temple. Oliver was closer to the rocks. He was lying on his side, much like the body they'd seen in his bed. Kneeling beside him, she put down her gun and reached to feel for a pulse at his neck. But though she pressed her fingers hard against his flesh, she felt no sign of life. After a long moment, she looked toward Singh.

The rebel leader and his men were also on the ground. Also unmoving. But as she started to stand, the Lion groaned. Raising his head, he stared directly at her, his dark eyes cloudy—yet fierce. A trickle of blood oozed from his mouth, but he pushed himself up. "You!" he gasped, bringing his gun up and toward her. "The wife of Satan."

"Don't. It's over."

"For everyone. For your husband. For you."

Eyes riveted to the muzzle of the machine gun, Abby slid her hand toward the weapon she'd laid beside Oliver.

From behind Singh, she caught a blur of motion. Steve! But everything was happening too fast. Or too slowly.

Steve barreled out of the temple at a dead run, heading for the Lion.

"Abby! For God's sake, get back. Get back!" he shouted.

Singh rolled to the side and began to swing his weapon around.

Changing directions, Steve sprinted toward the little mound of dirt where the closest guard lay sprawled. The man's machine gun was still strapped to his lifeless shoulder.

Throwing himself to the ground beside the body, Steve grabbed the weapon and tried to pull it into firing position. It was stuck under the corpse.

But Singh had given Abby the precious seconds she needed. She reached for the pistol she'd laid beside Oliver.

She didn't know who fired first—she or Singh. Or Steve. All she knew was that bullets spattered the ground around Singh and the body in front of Steve.

The clatter stopped as abruptly as it had started. The jungle was silent again. No one moved.

"Steve?" Heart blocking her windpipe, Abby sprinted past the now-lifeless bodies of the rebels.

Her husband pushed himself up. Then he was on his feet, running to meet her. They came together with a choked sob. Hers. And a fervent prayer of thanks. His.

Steve kissed her fiercely, as if he'd thought he might never see her again. And she returned the urgent pressure of his lips, hardly able to believe that he was really in her arms, alive. And well.

His hands cupped around her shoulders. "Abby, what are you doing here?"

"I couldn't let you do it. The Omega. I couldn't let you—"

"What about Shannon?" he cut in urgently.

"She's at Raj's house, with Noel. She's fine."

Steve let out a long, shuddering breath. "Noel's here? She came with Jason?"

"Yes."

"Then the temple should be decontaminated. At least I hope it is."

"It is. And the Omega's in there wrapped up tighter than a surprise package from the army special projects division."

They both whirled to see Jason and Raj standing on the road, both breathing hard, both with weapons drawn. The duo reholstered their pistols.

"And the interior of the temple has been chemically scrubbed. Although I'd guess that's not going to save any of the plants within a five-hundred-meter radius."

"So that's why it smelled to high heaven in there," Steve muttered.

"Jason. Thank you. Oh, thank you," Abby breathed, looking from him to Steve and back again.

"Yeah. It's been a busy forty-eight hours."

"I'm sorry we were away from home when you arrived," Raj told Abby. "I've had quite a bit of unexpected company lately."

"We got back from town, and Noel told us where you'd gone," Jason said. "I was afraid we were going to be too late. But I see you have things under control."

"Thanks to my Rambo wife," Steve interjected, pulling Abby more tightly against his side.

She clung to him. Now that the danger was over, she felt limp and shaky.

Steve stroked her back and shoulders as she struggled to keep from going to pieces in front of their friends.

"Let's get out of here," Jason said.

"Yeah." With an arm firmly around Abby, Steve began to lead her back down the road. Then he stopped and looked quizzically at the bodies in the clearing. "Singh. And the three guards," he muttered. "And someone else."

"Oliver," Abby whispered.

"That's impossible!"

"No," Raj told him. "The man you found in his bed was someone else."

"What?" Steve swung around to face the physician.

"The medical examiner was suspicious because of the skeletal development. It wasn't consistent with western nutritional standards, so he asked to see Oliver's medical records."

"Steve, I'm sorry," Abby murmured. "He's the one by the rocks. He showed up just before you and Singh. And . . . and he scared the wits out of me."

"I'll bet," Steve said slowly.

She took his hand, and his fingers tightened around hers.

"He told me the man in his bed was someone named Ari. He was the pilot who flew the Omega here."

"Ari. Yeah." Steve sighed.

"I'm sure Oliver was exposed, too," Abby said. "I think it affected his mind—his judgment. He wouldn't stay under cover. He was trying to save you from Singh. That's why he started shooting."

Steve's eyes were watery. "I'm sorry he ended up this way."

"I know," Abby whispered. At least Steve had already had time to come to terms with Oliver's death. He stared back at his friend for a long moment and was very quiet as the group made their way back to the vehicles.

But on the ride back to Raj's house, they had business to discuss.

"Someone's going to want to know how Amarjit Singh ended up dead out here," Jason muttered. "Not to mention what he was doing with a Russian chemical weapon that was supposed to have been destroyed."

"I'm way ahead of you," Steve told him. "It's not going to be our problem. There are a couple of CIA agents named Driscoll and McGuire who are going to be delighted to claim credit for the operation. And I just happen to have a twenty-four-hour number where I can reach them."

"I guess they can empty out Oliver's warehouse while they're at it," Abby said.

"Yeah. I was wondering who'd been in that box of grenades." Steve nodded at Jason. "I thought it might have been you."

"I looked through the stuff, but I didn't take anything."

"What about Tang Wu?" Abby asked.

"What about him?"

"Will he come after us?"

"Not if we use the same insurance policy I took out with Singh. Only this time it will be true. We'll write up an account of what happened and leave it in our safe-deposit box with instructions to deliver it to the CIA if something happens to us. We'll explain that to him when we send back his ring," Steve suggested.

Abby felt one more layer of worry lifted from her shoulders.

As soon as they reached the house, Noel, who must have been sitting by the window looking down the road, came flying out the door holding Shannon.

It was Steve who took the baby from her. With a catch in his breath, he closed his eyes and cradled the infant against his chest. Abby felt her heart contract as she watched Shannon snuggle against her father. Moving closer, she put her arms around the two of them, trembling as she thought about what might have happened. Peripherally she was aware that the others had gone inside, giving them privacy.

"Thank the Lord she's out of danger," Steve whispered, his hand delicately stroking the back of Shannon's head.

Abby covered his large hand with her smaller one. "I know. I'm trying to absorb that. We can go home now and be an ordinary family."

"Not quite ordinary," he whispered.

She looked up at him. "Are you thinking about Omega?"

"What if we can't—"

"The good Lord has given us one very wonderful little girl," she said before he could finish the question. "If that's all we're allowed, that will be enough for me."

Steve nodded, but his eyes were still troubled.

"What?" Abby asked.

He swallowed. "It's not something we can settle standing out here. Everybody's waiting for us."

"Let them wait." She made no move to enter the house, and the expectant silence stretched.

"All right," he finally said. "The whole time Singh had Shannon, I kept thinking that my past had come back to put my wife and child in danger. How do you feel about that?" He looked at her challengingly, and she felt her insides melt.

"Steve, you weren't responsible for a stupid decision Oliver made. Ever since I left Baltimore for India, all I've been thinking about was how much I needed you to help me get Shannon back."

He looked down at the baby in his arms. "You have her back. Now, are you sorry you married me?" he pressed.

"No!" Fiercely, she grabbed him by the shoulders. "Maybe I haven't been making myself understood. I need you. I love you. I want to spend the rest of my life with you."

The baby stirred in Steve's arms, and Abby automatically glanced down to check on her. One tiny fist was clenched tightly around a handful of Steve's shirt. As Abby watched, Shannon reached out the other hand and grabbed her mother's blouse.

Abby's vision misted as she looked down at their child. "Steve," she whispered, "Look."

He followed the direction of her gaze, staring at the tiny human bridge the baby had made between them.

"I think she's trying to tell us something," Abby whispered. She saw Steve swallow hard.

As if she understood the conversation, Shannon gave a little tug on her mother's blouse. With a shaky laugh, Abby moved a couple of inches closer to her husband and child. She put one hand on the baby's middle. The other stole around Steve's neck, tipping his head down toward hers.

Their eyes locked. Then their lips met. At first the kiss was like a bonding, more spiritual than carnal. But as Steve nibbled on her lower lip, Abby forgot where they were, forgot everything but him. A tiny fist pounding against her middle brought her down to earth.

"I think we'd better behave," Steve growled.

Abby pressed her knuckles against his cheek. "I love you so much. And I heard what you said to Singh outside the temple."

"I didn't know you were eavesdropping."

"Well, I was, so you can't take it back. Shannon and I won't let you."

He looked from his daughter to his wife. "Are the two of you ganging up on me?"

"Yeah."

His hand gently touched the baby's face and then Abby's.

"God, you're something. You're both really something."

Abby tried to blink away the moisture brimming in her eyes. "We both love you, too. A lot," she whispered.

"I thanked you once for giving me this," Steve choked out.

"And I told you we'd done it together."

"I'll keep that in mind."

"That's all I'm asking," she told him, sighing contentedly as she relaxed into his embrace.

And there's more 43 LIGHT STREET!

Turn the page for a bonus look at what's in store in WHAT CHILD IS THIS?, Rebecca York's next 43 Light Street tale.

In the hallowed halls of this charming building you've seen danger averted and romance blossom. Now Christmas comes to 43 Light Street and in its stocking is all the action, suspense and romance you've come to expect from Rebecca York.

Chapter One

Guilty until proven innocent.

Erin Morgan squinted into the fog that turned the buildings on either side of Light Street into a canyon of dimly realized apparitions.

"Guilty until proven innocent," she repeated aloud.

It wasn't supposed to work that way. Yet that was how Erin had felt since the Graveyard Murders had rocked Baltimore. Ever since the killer had tricked her into framing her friend Sabrina Barkley.

Sabrina had forgiven her. But she hadn't forgiven herself, and she was never going to let something like that happen again.

She glanced at the purse beside her on the passenger seat and felt her stomach knot. It was stuffed with five thousand dollars in contributions for Santa's Toy and Clothing Fund. Most were checks, but she was carrying more than eight hundred dollars in cash. And she wasn't going to keep it in her possession a moment longer than necessary.

Erin pressed her foot down on the accelerator and then eased up again as a dense patch of white swallowed up the car. She couldn't even see the Christmas decorations she knew were festooned from many of the downtown office windows.

"'Tis the season to be jolly...." She sang a few lines of the carol to cheer herself up, but her voice trailed off in the gloom.

Forty-three Light Street glided into view through the mist like a huge underwater rock formation.

Erin drove around to the back of the building where she could get in and out as quickly as possible. Pulling the collar of her coat closed against the icy wind, she hurried toward the back door—the key ready in her hand.

It felt good to get out of the cold. But there was nothing welcoming about the dank, dimly lit back entrance—so different from the fading grandeur of the marble foyer. Here there were no pretensions of gentility, only institutional gray walls and a bare concrete floor.

Clutching her purse more tightly, she strained her ears and peered into the darkness. She heard nothing but the familiar sound of the steam pipes rattling. And she saw nothing moving in the shadows. Still, the fine hairs on the back of her neck stirred as she bolted into the service elevator and pressed the button.

Upstairs the paint was brighter, and the tile floors were polished. But at this time of night, only a few dim lights held back the shadows, and the clicking of her high heels echoed back at her like water dripping in an underground cavern.

Feeling strangely exposed in the darkness, Erin kept her eyes focused on the glass panel of her office door. She was almost running by the time she reached it.

Her hand closed around the knob. It was solid and reassuring against her moist palm, and she felt some of the knots in her stomach untie themselves. With a sigh of relief, she kicked the door closed behind her, shutting out the unseen phantoms of the hall.

Reaching over one of the mismatched couches donated by a local rental company, she flipped the light switch. Nothing happened. Darn. The bulb must be out.

In the darkness, she took a few steps toward the file room and stopped.

Something else was wrong. Maybe it was the smell. Not the clean pine scent of the little Christmas tree she'd set up by the window, but the dank odor of sweat.

She was backing quietly toward the door when fingers as hard and lean as a handcuff shot out and closed around her wrist.

A scream of terror rose in her throat. The sound was choked off by a rubber glove against her lips.

Someone was in her office. In the dark.

Her mind registered no more than that. But her body was already struggling—trying to twist away.

"No. Please." Even as she pleaded, she knew she was wasting her breath.

He was strong. And ruthless.

Her free hand came up to pummel his shoulder and neck. He grunted and shook her so hard that her vision blurred.

She tried to work her teeth against the rubbery palm that covered her mouth.

His grip adroitly shifted to her throat. He began to squeeze, and she felt the breath turn to stone in her lungs.

He bent her backward over his arm, and she stared up into a face covered by a ski mask, the features a strange parody of something human.

The dark circles around the eyes—the red circle around the mouth, the two dots of color on his cheeks—wavered in her vision like coins in the bottom of a fountain.

The pressure increased. Her lungs were going to explode.

No. Please. Let me go home. I have a little boy. He needs me.

The words were choked off like her life breath.

Like the rapidly fading light. She was dying. And the scenes of her life flashed before her eyes. Climbing into bed with her parents on Sunday morning. First grade. High school graduation. Her marriage to Bruce. Kenny's birth. Her husband's death. Betraying Sabrina. Finishing college. Her new job with Silver Miracle Charities. The holiday fund-raiser tonight.

The events of her life trickled through her mind like the last grains of sand rolling down the sloping sides of an hourglass. Then there was only blackness.

* * * * *

Don't miss the next 43 Light Street tale—
What Child Is This? *coming December 1993—
from Rebecca York and Harlequin Intrigue!*

THREE UNFORGETTABLE HEROINES
THREE AWARD-WINNING AUTHORS

MAVERICK HEARTS

A unique collection of historical short stories that capture the spirit of America's last frontier.

HEATHER GRAHAM POZZESSERE—over 10 million copies of her books in print worldwide
Lonesome Rider—The story of an Eastern widow and the renegade half-breed who becomes her protector.

PATRICIA POTTER—an author whose books are consistently Waldenbooks bestsellers
Against the Wind—Two people, battered by heartache, prove that love can heal all.

JOAN JOHNSTON—award-winning Western historical author with 17 books to her credit
One Simple Wish—A woman with a past discovers that dreams really do come true.

Join us for an exciting journey West with
UNTAMED
Available in July, wherever Harlequin books are sold.

Hop into a pink Cadillac with the King of Rock 'n' Roll for the
hottest—most mysterious—August of 1993 ever!

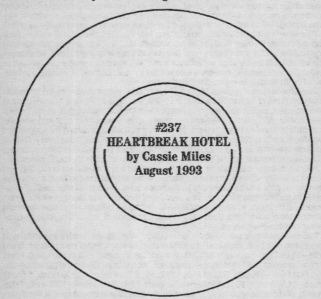

#237
HEARTBREAK HOTEL
by Cassie Miles
August 1993

All Susan Quentin wanted was a quiet birthday, but she got
lots more: sexy greetings over the radio, deejay Johnny Swift
himself—and a dead Elvis impersonator outside her door.
Armed with only sunglasses and a pink Cadillac, could they
find the disguised "King" killer amid a convention of
impersonators at the Heartbreak Hotel?

Don't be cruel! Come along for the ride of your life when
Johnny tries to convince Susan to love him tender!   ELVIS